how to lose a bachelor

ANNA
BANKS

Entangled Publishing, LLC
2614 South Timberline Road
Suite 109
Fort Collins, CO 80525
Visit our website at www.entangledpublishing.com.

Bliss is an imprint of Entangled Publishing, LLC. For more information on our titles, visit http://www.entangledpublishing.com/category/bliss

Edited by Liz Pelletier
Cover design by Heather Howland
Cover art from iStock

Manufactured in the United States of America

First Edition October 2015

Bliss

For my sister Tami, who loved the idea, but never got to read the story.

Chapter One

Rochelle Ransom hadn't worn a dress like this since... actually, she'd never worn a dress like this. Short, tight, lots of cleavage. Hooker red. Any judge would kick her out of the courtroom if she traipsed in looking like this, hauling a briefcase and with a mortified client trailing behind her. Of course, she'd never make it to the bench. Not in these ankle-breaking stilettos.

But this wasn't a courtroom. This was the set—or rather, the dining room of a humongous mansion—of *Luring Love*, the reality show she'd signed up for six months ago. Oh, at first, she'd thought it was funny that the show was auditioning in her city. She thought women had to be desperate to put themselves out there like that, and chase after a man. The last thing she needed in life right now was a man interfering with her career and the time she spent working for her favorite charity, Helping Hands. But as the audition date drew near, she began to think of a very good reason to try out. Of course, there was the prospect of meeting an attractive man who was probably only interested in sex (and Rochelle's sex life was nonexistent), but there was also the exposure on national television for Helping Hands, and the prize money if she actually won the show. Yep, she was all in when she realized the possibilities. She could sacrifice some pride in order to raise funds for a good cause couldn't she? Of course she could. And so, after dozens of interviews and near-painful home videos outlining the very boring details of her life, she'd somehow made it as a finalist. She was going to be on TV. But more importantly, nothing was going to stop her from winning the grand prize money for her charity.

Oh yeah, and the bachelor's heart or whatever.

But seriously, the winnings would free up time to take on the cases that meant something to her—instead of all the time she wasted making rich corporations even richer. Sure, being a corporate attorney paid the bills but representing penniless, battered women who came through Helping Hands was her real passion. After most grueling workdays, she would head over to give the last of her energy to the incredible women staying there. It was a shelter without other connections or financial options, and she would often find herself rotating between the roles of pro bono legal advisor, amateur therapist, and housekeeper depending on the daily needs and demands.

Becoming a contestant on this show put her in a better position to meet those needs and demands.

It was a shallow means to a worthy end. Her closest girlfriends could tease her all they wanted about "ulterior motives" but Rochelle stubbornly refuted them. This was NOT about finding love. That ship had sailed—and sunk and was rotting on the ocean floor.

She took a generous sip of champagne, wondering how many times she'd have to tell herself that over the course of the next twelve weeks. *I'm whoring myself out for money, after all.* She'd never even seen an episode of *Luring Love*, but she'd overheard her assistant Jennifer and her paralegal Gemini talking about past seasons, and the word "scandalous" came up every few sentences or so. Who slept with whom. Who threw a colossal temper tantrum and got voted off. Who had the bikini "mishap." (Apparently there was always a bikini mishap.)

One thing she had already decided, though, was that there was no way she was sleeping with the guy. He was lucky enough to have all these women vying for his attention, but to expect them all to sleep with him, too? *You've got to be freaking kidding me. We might as well inject ourselves with an STD cocktail.*

But all else was fair game. Charm him, wine and dine him. She was even willing to do her own version of a bikini mishap in order to rouse his, er, heart—or at least, borrow his affection for the duration of the show. Maybe after the show, they could even be friends. As long as she could talk him out of his half of the prize money.

Heh.

Either way, this poor guy didn't stand a chance. Jennifer and Gemini saw to it that she knew all the ways to win his heart and all the ways to avoid getting voted off the show. If there was one thing Rochelle had cornered the market on, it was persuasiveness. Her track record in the circuit court system was evidence enough of that. How hard could romancing a bachelor be, anyway?

A man was a man was a man. They were all the same. Clean-shaven sasquatches dressed in suits and ties.

She glanced around the room with a self-satisfied grin and began sizing up the competition as she sipped her champagne. And her confidence abruptly faltered. She was the least attractive out of the entire bunch—and that was *after* she'd put more effort into her appearance than ever before.

Oh crap. The nine other women were nothing short of gorgeous, each in their own way. And "gorgeous" was something Rochelle had never considered herself. Not even now, in her prostitute uniform.

But the one who worried Rochelle the most was the tall woman who lingered shyly in the corner, acting oblivious to the fact that she was the most striking female in the room. Long, straight black hair. Smooth, dewy skin the color of a perfectly crafted cappuccino. Legs that went on for decades, and lips that formed a perfect come-hither pout without even trying.

I'm so screwed. Rochelle took an unfeminine gulp of her drink, downing the last of her champagne and motioning for another. The waiter paused as she switched out the empty glass for a full one on his tray. Down the hatch it went.

The waiter gave her a startled look. "No need to be nervous," he whispered in an Australian accent. "He's actually quite nice."

"Who?" Why would he think she was nervous? Didn't everyone, on occasion, guzzle champagne?

"The Bachelor." The waiter turned on his heel. "I think you'll find him to be decent."

"Oh. Right." The Bachelor. The poor sucker who was about to be subjected to irresistible temptation by the sumptuous Nubian princess over in the corner. *I might as well go home.*

And that was when she realized why she had been chosen for the show. Someone had to represent the ninety-nine percent of women who didn't make the cut for this show.

Oh God.

The waiter left, making his way around the room, catering to all the other women who probably were well aware Rochelle was there for a quota, but didn't have a clue they were about to lose this competition to the shy black woman in the corner.

After the second glass of champagne kicked in, Rochelle decided to be proactive. And why shouldn't she? After all, she had more to lose than these other women. Attracting rich bachelors was probably just their hobby. Risking her life in the six-inch stilettos, she eased her way around the dining table, hobbling in the heels like a newborn calf, one graceless step at a time, until she reached the hands-down winner of *Luring Love.*

"Hi," she told the princess. *Even I'm irritated by how perky I sound.* In fact, she was usually allergic to perky people herself—especially before 9 a.m. and two cappuccinos—but she suspected dry sarcasm wasn't going to win her any points on the show or with the beauty queen standing next to her. It wasn't wise to piss anyone off just yet, because her assistant had told her—over and over again—that would be asking for immediate sabotage by the other contestants. So perky it was. "I'm Rochelle." *I'm here to represent the normal Americans who couldn't make it today.*

The princess smiled, revealing the teeth of a dentist's daughter. *Of course.* "I'm Maya," she replied. "I like your dress." Maya swirled the champagne in her glass. "Are you nervous? Because I'm about to pass out."

So Maya was lovely and honest. "Don't be nervous. The waiter tells me our bachelor is a nice guy. So, no need to poison him just yet." *Oops, too morbid.*

But the other woman laughed. "Honestly, I'm more nervous about the competition. He's just a man, right? But look at you, for instance. You're rocking your dress. And have you seen the twins? What's up with that?"

Lovely, honest, and humble. *Triple threat, which means I'm doubly screwed.* "They're really twins, you think?"

"I know so. I asked."

"So if one of them wins…"

"Awkward."

Yep, she officially liked Maya. Which wasn't good, since she was going to have to be ruthless in getting her voted off. Preferably first.

Just then, the producer, Richie Odom, a buttery-smooth-talking man with a slicked-back hairpiece—and an ego the size of a tank—interrupted Rochelle's strategizing. Holding up both his hands, which revealed that his tacky red velvet jacket was a bit too short in the sleeves, he announced, "Okay, ladies, we're about to start filming. The bachelor is going to enter through the door behind me. When he does, I want you to act naturally. Do whatever pops up first into your head when you see him—which I hope looks a lot like insta-love googly eyes. Remember, there are ten of you and only three cameramen, so if we're going to get a shot of his first impression of you, you'll have to hold your pose—in the most natural way possible, of course. Remember, this is a reality show. Everything is real. So make sure real looks good." He consulted the stopwatch in his hand. "We've got a twenty-second countdown."

"Here we go," Maya whispered.

Rochelle took the opportunity to swap out another empty glass of champagne for a full one from the waiter's tray as he passed by. He shot her a disapproving look but continued on his way. *Yeah, that's right. Keep walking. You're not the one about to trade your dignity for cash.*

"Ten seconds!" Richie yelled.

All eyes focused on the entryway, waiting for the moment when the small talk would end and the rivalry would begin. The second that Bachelor hit the door, he'd be the center of attention for the next twelve weeks.

And for the next twelve weeks, Rochelle was going to have to be perky. Likable. Non-snarky.

Think of the money, think of the money, think of the money.

"Five seconds!"

Four.

Three.

Two.

One.

Rochelle hadn't realized she'd been holding her breath—until Grant Drake stepped through the entryway. Then she let it out in a heaving gasp.

And her champagne glass plummeted to the floor.

Chapter Two

They had instructed Grant to smile at each and every bachelorette in the room, at least long enough to give the camera a slight reaction. But his attention immediately fixated on the sound of shattering glass—and on the woman who stood in a puddle of champagne and glass shards.

Rochelle Ransom.

The woman who'd stormed out of his life like an all-consuming hurricane.

He would have been a jackass if he'd asked her to stay in Florida after she'd been accepted to Berkeley. As it turned out, he'd acted like a jackass anyway. But what had she expected? She'd applied for Berkeley behind his back and suddenly sprang it on him at the dinner—where he was going to propose—that she was leaving for the west coast. Of course he'd been mad. And, all truth told, he'd been destroyed, too.

Now he was going to have to relive it all over again in order to get his vengeance.

Maybe this wasn't such a good idea after all.

The producers of the show had outdone themselves this time, sifting through hundreds of applicants, trying to find perfect matches for one lucky bachelor. To him, Rochelle Ransom was, and always would be, his perfect match. Obviously, the casting director of *Luring Love* agreed with him. That guy deserved a special crevice in hell.

But God, Rochelle was still a knockout. Red had always been her color, but stilettos? He'd never seen her flaunt her assets like this, not even at college parties. The way her dress clung to her every curve like static electricity, how the halter exposed the corresponding perfection of her breasts. They may not have been the largest pair in the room, but he remembered vividly how they'd felt in his hands. How good they'd felt pressed against his bare chest.

And she couldn't have picked a better shade of red lipstick. Lips that knew just exactly how to make him growl with pleasure.

Yes, she was the most tempting thing in the room, by far. The lust shooting straight through him was evidence enough of that.

Still, it made him furious, all of it. *She always dressed in T-shirts and jeans for me, and now she's dressed like a supermodel in hopes of tempting some joker on a reality show to marry her?*

Then he remembered—*he* was that joker. And this reality show could be his chance for revenge. After all, his friend just *happened* to be the show's host, Chris Legend, who helped get him on in the first place. This had to work. In theory, it had sounded brilliant. But by the withering look Rochelle was giving him, he only had it half right. He was a joker—but this might not be a chance at vengeance.

Richie Odom was about to make things much, much worse, he could tell. "You two, come with me. Now."

The grand, elegant set of *Luring Love* erupted in whispers and pointing as he followed Rochelle and Richie out of the room.

Chapter Three

How many times can Grant Drake ruin my life?

Rochelle took the seat next to him in front of Richie's desk, unwilling to look in his direction. Instead, she let her eyes wander everywhere else, taking in the majestic gentility of the mansion's library, which Richie had obviously claimed as his personal office space. Books lined each of the walls, and the shelves were adorned with tracks for a rickety-looking sliding ladder—a reader's paradise. A hint of stale cigar smoke wafted in the air, lending the room a distinctly male atmosphere.

She scooted her chair as far away from Grant as possible before fixing her gaze on the flustered producer in front of her.

"You two know each other. How?" Richie leaned to the side of his high-backed office chair, drumming his fingers impatiently on the giant desk. It reminded her of the many times she had been called into the dean's office at university.

Who knew debating a professor's view on every single subject was a mortal sin?

She didn't know how to answer Richie's question. Not like a lady, anyway. She certainly didn't want to re-hash their story to anyone, especially a snide producer who wouldn't understand insignificant things such as feelings and pride and random urges to attack the man sitting next to her.

She stopped herself cold. Feelings? The only feelings she had left for Grant Drake were borderline murderous—right? *So why are my insides whirling like a tornado?*

Grant wasn't talking, either. Probably too ashamed of himself. And rightly so. He'd stolen her heart and then river-danced on it with cleats. The thought of it made her nearly choke on the fiery bile erupting from her stomach.

Her insides screamed at her, *What's the deal? Why am I letting him affect me this way?* For the past ten years, she had successfully suppressed all the anger and hurt he'd caused, never letting it bubble to the surface, never letting it affect her life, her career. Sure, there had been a time when she'd thought Grant was The One. That was before he'd abruptly ended their relationship just when she was going to ask him to take it to the next level. Just when she was going to ask him to up and move with her to the west coast after she got accepted to Berkeley.

But Rochelle had risen above all that, the pain and humiliation. She had picked herself up from the proverbial floor, finished college, then law school, and went on to start an amazing career. At twenty-nine, she was in a prime position to make partner soon. She'd worked her butt off, finding strength in the fact that she could leave the past in the past. That she could overcome insignificant obstacles like Grant

Drake.

Heck, she had become an obstacle-devouring beast.

Except that now, with the insignificant obstacle himself sitting a few feet away from her, she felt like a certifiable lunatic on the verge of a meltdown. And "meltdown" was not in her vocabulary.

"I'm waiting," Richie said after what seemed like an eternity.

Grant cleared his throat. "Chelle and I—"

"Do not call me Chelle." Grant was the only person who ever called her Chelle, and she used to love it. Now she despised the sound of it on his lips—and what it did to her heartbeat.

Out of the corner of her eye, she saw Grant pause and look at her. He recovered quickly, just like he always had. Calm, collected Grant. Except when she unleashed her tongue on certain parts of his body.

Stop that. Immediately.

"Rochelle and I dated in college," Grant continued, oblivious. "We… Things were left on bad terms."

Bad terms? Understatement of the millennium. Still, she was glad he didn't want to restate the facts. The facts could still drive her mad to this day. She remembered the way he'd broken up with her. His indifference. No, she didn't want to relive that. She couldn't bear to hear him say he'd fallen out of love with her. Not again.

Richie watched them closely, pressing his fingertips together. "So you two have a colorful past."

"Imagine the rainbow and all the colors in between," she said.

The corner of Richie's mouth tugged up. "Still hard

feelings, I see."

"It was a difficult breakup," Grant said diplomatically.

She shot him an "are-you-serious" glare, before looking back at Richie. "I assume this disqualifies me from the show. I'm happy to take my leave."

She started to rise, but Richie held out his hand. "Not necessarily, Ms. Ransom."

"Actually it does. I'm an attorney, Mr. Odom. I read contracts carefully. It specifically says—"

"Grant, could you excuse us for just a moment?" Richie said. "I'd like to discuss the circumstances with Ms. Ransom privately."

"Of course." Since when was Grant the epitome of politeness? But she recognized the wariness in his voice. *He probably doesn't want me to relate all the morbid details of that night. Rest assured, I won't, Grant Drake. I don't want to relive it either.*

After Grant closed the door behind him, Richie offered her a sympathetic smile. "I can't imagine what you must be going through right now."

She raised her chin just a bit. "I'm fine."

"With all due respect, Ms. Ransom, you don't look fine. I mean, you dropped your champagne glass when you saw Grant walk through the door."

"I was shocked to see him. Surely you can understand that?" She'd been shocked and outraged and in need of something more stout than a swallow or two of champagne.

Richie leaned back, assessing her. She didn't like the look in his eyes. Richie Odom might have been the dense, Hollywood type, but she'd seen this kind of calculating expression before—and it was usually worn by defense attorneys right before they sprang a surprise witness on the courtroom, or requested to admit a piece of evidence that hadn't been previously discussed.

Something despicable had unfurled in Richie's little brain, she could tell. And she hoped he'd reveal his intentions soon. She had a cab to catch to the airport, after all.

After a few more moments of scrutiny, Richie said, "Why did you try out for *Luring Love*, Ms. Ransom? And don't tell me you did it to find true love. No one in their right mind resorts to a dating show for that nonsense."

"You don't believe in what you're selling?"

He ignored her question, instead sifting through pages on the thin tablet in his hand. She knew what he was looking for when he pressed an index finger on the screen then opened his hand to widen the view. He took a long moment to read, probably just to keep her in suspense. "You're a successful corporate attorney, which at your age, means you're an over-achiever. You definitely don't have time for love, do you, Ms. Ransom?"

"I have a strong work ethic." But he had nailed it, and they both knew it. She worked twelve-hour days during the week, then took her work home with her on the weekends. She barely had time to brush her teeth.

He read another page. "You've already made a name for yourself in the court circuit, and you apparently have more work than you can handle, so you're definitely not on the show for more publicity. Let's see here…" He scanned through a few screens, then paused on one. "Ah-ha. You volunteer at Helping Hands women's shelter. Oh, you're the president! Trying to bring attention to your cause, then? A warrior against domestic violence?"

Maybe, but she still wanted to punch him in the face right then. "You could say that."

He pursed his lips, then opened the laptop on his desk and plucked at the keyboard. After a few seconds, he turned back to her, facing the laptop in her direction. "It says here that Helping Hands is trying to raise money for a new housing facility in a better part of town. You're in it for the grand prize money, Ms. Ransom. You're going to donate it, aren't you?"

"Which, if I remember correctly, also disqualifies me from the show." The contract had specified that the contestant must be emotionally and physically available to find their soul mate in order to participate in the show. The grand prize money was intended strictly for the couple's enjoyment—wedding, vacation, honeymoon, and other senseless things. A fact that, until now, Rochelle was confident she could talk her way out of. If the bachelor was any kind of decent man, he'd readily agree to donate the money. But she knew how decent Grant Drake wasn't. And she just wanted to get out of here and on with her life—again. How long would it take her this time? Would she mourn? Would she gain weight by eating all the ice cream she could get her hands on? She wasn't as young as she had been when he'd ruined her life the first time. This time, the threat of cellulite was very real.

"You don't want to be on the show anymore."

"You think?"

"What I think is that you should stay on the show. You have such a worthy cause, after all. And there's definitely still chemistry between you two."

"Stay? Are you crazy? We're about as chemically

compatible as potassium and water." Which exploded upon contact with each other, if she remembered correctly. Against her will, she recalled just how explosive they could be together, she and Grant. Having studied every inch of her body like a final exam, Grant Drake used to keep her moaning for hours.

"What if Mr. Drake is a changed man? He strikes me as a nice guy."

She rolled her eyes. "You're wasting your time and mine with that one. Why are you trying to keep me on the show? We know each other. It's a direct violation of the contract."

He waved in dismissal. "Contract, schmontract. That's for the legal department." Leaning forward in the chair, he folded his hands in front of him. "I'm a producer, Ms. Ransom. My job is to earn ratings. Do you know what gets the highest ratings?"

"Love?"

"Drama."

He wants to exploit our relationship. My agony. My heartbreak. All for ratings.

She stood. "This discussion is over."

Richie rose, too. "I'll double the prize money. Personally. No one will have to know. Think of what that will do for Helping Hands."

She drew in a deep breath. Double the prize money? "You're assuming Grant will choose me, Mr. Odom. You're asking me to stay and play a game of chance. One that I've already lost in the past." It hurt worse than she thought it would to say that out loud.

"You were already going to play the game before any- way, right? Why let Grant Drake change that? You're doing it for a great cause. Besides, it's not like you still have feelings for the guy. You're in no danger there, correct?"

She couldn't help but scowl, even as her stomach did flips. "Of course not."

"I'll make a deal with you. You don't have to win. If you just *stay* on the show, I'll give you double the prize money. Your only obligation is not to quit."

"I would love to take advantage of your stupidity, Mr. Odom, but I have a conscience. Grant will vote me off the show the first chance he gets. That means you're doubling the prize money for one episode of precious drama. Not the best deal for you."

"But what if he doesn't vote you off? He didn't seem like he had any ill will toward you."

"I keyed his 1969 Ford Mustang. Then set fire to his mother's house." Well, that last part had been an accident. She'd gone to his mother's to pick up a box of her things he'd left there for her, and caught his fourteen-year-old sister smoking in her bedroom. She'd slapped the cigarette out of her hand, and…homework burned particularly fast, she'd learned.

At this, Richie Odom's mouth formed a definitive O. Sure, he was shocked, but Rochelle could tell he was also delighted. To him, the more she said, the higher the ratings rocketed.

Disgusting.

"I want you on the show. Period. If he votes you off on the first episode, then lucky you."

Slowly, she sat back down. "You're telling me that as long as I don't quit, you'll give me the prize money? Even if he votes me off?"

"No. I'm telling you that I'll give you *double* the prize money. Even if he votes you off. You just can't quit. That's the only stipulation."

"He already broke up with me, Mr. Odom."

"Drama, Ms. Ransom."

She imagined all the things Helping Hands could do with that money. They'd have a new building, new furniture to go with it. They could even start up their own low-cost daycare, to help battered working mothers get back on their feet. It had been something the committee had talked about—no, dreamed about—but it always seemed out of reach, especially with their puny budget.

How can I say no?

Richie was right. Why let the likes of Grant Drake stand in the way of such a worthy cause? *Helping Hands needs that money—who am I not to try?* It was only twelve weeks of her saved up paid vacation—she had to use it or lose it anyway. And deep down, she knew she would lose it. Still, just thinking of all the work she could get done on a staycation nestled in bed with her laptop and a glass of wine had her almost salivating.

The word "workaholic" was invented for people like her.

So I'll do everything in my power to get voted off the first week. How hard can it be?

She offered Richie her most insincere smile. "You have a deal, Mr. Odom."

Chapter Four

Grant shut the door behind him and strode to Richie's extravagant mahogany desk. The producer looked pleased with himself—which put Grant instantly on guard. If there was one thing he'd learned about Richie Odom during the bachelor selection process, it was that the man could only be gratified at the expense of others.

"Mr. Drake, please do sit," Richie said.

As soon as he did, he felt an emptiness in the chair beside him, where *she'd* been sitting, just an hour ago. Even now, he could smell her perfume lingering in the air. And to be honest, he was still reeling from the sight of her, too.

"I just wanted to let you know that Ms. Ransom has decided to stay on the show."

Grant's blood thickened in his veins. *She's staying?* "How did you manage to pull that off?" He was proud of himself for keeping his voice at a manly octave.

Richie shrugged. "I'm sure you know Ms. Ransom to be

a reasonable person. I simply threatened her with the contract she signed. In signing that dotted line, she promised she would do everything she could to win the bachelor's heart. Which would be you, like it or not. You did hear her say she's an attorney, yes? She knows it's all legally binding."

"I also heard her say that staying on the show is illegal. Because of our history."

Richie remained unfazed. "I showed her specific wording in the contract where we could get around that little snafu. If, of course, we let it go to court. Which she doesn't want to happen. It would be a conflict of interest, you see, for an attorney to get sued."

Grant imagined that attorneys got sued all the time. "That woman hates me. She wouldn't stay because of a contract." Of that he was certain. If there was anything he knew about Chelle, it was that she upheld her principles — no matter the cost. He remembered that last painful dinner together. He'd just explained to her all the reasons their relationship no longer worked, except of course for the *real* reason — that she was running off to the west coast without him. She proceeded to dump a plate full of spaghetti in his lap, rinsing it off with the remaining contents of her wine glass. Then she'd destroyed the new paint job on his car in the parking lot on her way out of his life.

"I wouldn't say that she hates you, per se —"

"She keyed my Camaro."

"I heard it was a Mustang."

Grant rolled his eyes. "She always got them confused."

"Nonetheless, she's staying. Congratulations! Now you can win her back."

"*Win her back?* You can count her as good as voted

off." Richie had just made it possible to do exactly that. Win Rochelle back after she'd announced her intention to move across the country to go to Berkeley law school and leave him behind? No way. The humiliation still stung his pride—and he felt a certain pang somewhere in the vicinity of his chest.

"I saw the way you looked at her. You're still in love with her." When Grant's mouth fell open, Richie smirked. "I'm a producer, Grant. It's my job to see things from different angles."

If Richie saw it, then what did Chelle see? *If she's an attorney, probably everything*. He nearly groaned. Of course he was still in love with her. But it didn't mean he wanted her here. It didn't mean he wanted to go down that path with her again. "You won't be so confident when I vote her off, I assure you."

Richie studied him. "Did you know I personally had a hand in picking you for this show?"

That caught Grant off guard. He shook his head. *Can't wait to hear this*. The only person responsible for his being on the show was Chris Schnartz-Legend. His longtime friend had seen an opening and acted on it. How much Richie had been involved in the decision, Grant wasn't sure.

"When Chris brought you to us, I told the studio that you were our guy. I said, 'This guy's a tactical training consultant. He'll be methodical, develop strategies. Bring America to its knees.' I told them you're a take-charge kind of man."

First of all, Grant doubted they even had another option on such short notice. Secondly, he could recognize false flattery when he heard it. Richie was buttering him up for something. The question was, what? "You gathered all that from a conversation with Chris? How profound. I'm a consultant, Richie, not a celebrity."

"A *consultant*? Don't be modest. People put their lives in your hands every time they hire you. The safety and protection of their children, their loved ones."

He shrugged. Maybe his techniques saved lives...if his clients had the sense to listen to him. "I teach them to defend themselves. Thanks for the vote of confidence, though."

But Richie was too self-absorbed to notice Grant's cynicism. "Don't you see? I've given you a second chance. You have twelve weeks to win Rochelle over, Grant. Isn't that what you want?"

"No."

"No?" Richie made a tsking sound with his tongue. "I thought we were being honest here. Man to man."

"You don't understand. Chelle—*Rochelle*—is the most stubborn woman alive. Pride is her specialty." That, and starting house fires.

"I persuaded her to stay, didn't I? Surely you could do the same. You're an attractive, successful man. You saw the faces of all those women when you entered the room, didn't you? You didn't disappoint the ladies, my friend. You're a catch, Grant. A stud. I even heard one of them use the term 'eye candy.'"

Grant nearly grimaced at the word "stud." How far would Richie go with his cheesy adulation to get his way? Besides, the only face Grant remembered seeing when he walked into the room was Chelle's. And she'd looked traumatized. Which made his confidence fizzle like a balloon with the air let out—and his heart pound like a machine gun.

"Besides," Richie continued, "she can't leave without

breeching the contract, which she doesn't want to do. The only way she can go anywhere now is if you vote her off. Think about all the power that gives you. She's at your mercy. How often does that happen?"

At my mercy. That does have a nice ring to it. Still, if anything, he was at *her* mercy—considering the way his body reacted to her just sitting next to him. Even after ten years, that aspect of their relationship hadn't changed.

But Richie was right. He had twelve whole weeks to make Rochelle miserable—why stop at just one? She deserved it, didn't she? She obviously wanted off the show; all he had to do to piss her off was keep her there. *Then* he'd vote her off. It was the perfect revenge.

Yes, the world would be watching. But maybe that was a good thing. After all, Chelle could be unpredictable at times. Surely she wouldn't try anything crazy in front of the cameras though.

Or would she?

Chapter Five

Rochelle placed her empty suitcase in the walk-in closet she now shared with Maya. She had originally been assigned to room with one of the twins, but they both pitched royalty-level fits so bedrooms were rearranged to accommodate them. No doubt an early strategic move on their part; rooming together gave them more time to scheme.

Not that I care. I don't have to beat them. I don't have to beat anyone. In fact, I intend to get voted off this week. And walk away with double the prize money.

She couldn't help but smile to herself in the wardrobe mirror. It was a small feat to swindle Hollywood.

"I never saw someone so happy to be in jeans before," Maya said from the doorway of the closet.

Rochelle laughed. "I do love my jeans." She turned to her new friend and crossed her arms. "You don't think our esteemed bachelor will mind, do you?"

Maya pressed her lips together. "What went down with

you two today anyway? You acted like you knew each other. What did Richie say?"

Uh-oh. She should've cooked up a solid story with Richie before she left his office. Now she was on her own. "I thought Grant was my cousin."

"Say what?"

Rochelle nodded emphatically. "He looks just like one of my cousins who lives in Georgia. For a second there, I thought I had signed up to date the kid who used to beat me up. It was awful. Glad that mess is over with." Somehow she'd have to relay that little lie to Richie. God only knew what he'd already come up with to explain things. She probably should have just asked for a directive on what to say, in case anyone questioned her behavior.

But Rochelle wasn't used to waiting around for instruction. *Sometimes you've just got to improvise.*

"Well, that was probably way creepy for you," Maya offered. She stepped inside the closet and started skimming through her wardrobe. All her clothes were name brand. In fact, it looked like a Paris runway threw up on her side of the walk-in. "We have makeup in an hour for the dinner filming. I hope they don't make us look like prostitutes."

"So you're saying my jeans are probably a no go." Maya may have dropped the subject, but Rochelle could tell she wasn't completely sold on the whole cousin story. It seemed as though she was just tucking the information away for a rainy day.

Rochelle could practically hear her assistant Jennifer whisper "gameplay." Maybe if she was actually staying in this competition, it might have mattered to her. But right now she couldn't care less. After tonight, Grant would want to send her packing.

"They said semi-formal. But don't worry about it. I'm sure the wardrobe people will help you find something… suitable," Maya was saying.

Rochelle gave herself a big grin in the mirror. "I'm sure they'll try," she muttered under her breath.

Rochelle twirled around and around in the makeup chair in front of the mirror, delighted beyond measure with herself. The wardrobe assistant, Shelley, had been no match for her; Rochelle had refused to change out of her rancid sweatshirt and no amount of coaxing on Shelley's part could change her mind. Exasperated, Shelley had gone to get help, poor thing. But no matter who showed up—even if it was Richie himself—Rochelle would be attending dinner in stinky casual attire. And she dared Richie to try to stop her.

Beside her in the next makeup chair over, a pretty woman with copper-toned skin and large, observant green eyes watched Rochelle, arrogance upturning her nose. "Darling," the woman said, "you do realize they're just trying to help you? Please take note that I am one of the contestants, and as such, I expect adequate competition."

Rochelle nearly laughed. The makeup room grew quiet. Even the makeup artists buzzed around silently tending to their charges. A lone cameraman filmed the process, probably for potential drama. He'd been focused on Rochelle ever since she'd thrown a fit when ordered to change into a gown.

"I don't need any help," Rochelle said. "If the bachelor can't accept me for who I am, then I don't want him."

"Utter nonsense," the woman scoffed. "A hobo wouldn't accept you looking and smelling like that. You think you're the only one who wants to be accepted? That is not how the world works, darling. Do you not recognize who *I* am?"

When Rochelle shook her head, the woman rolled her eyes, her expression full of disdain. "I'm Grace Le Fevre, heiress to the third largest fortune in this country. Do you really think anyone will ever want me for who I am, instead of for my fortune? Of course not. But I've learned to accept it. You should try to do the same."

Actually, Rochelle had heard of Grace Le Fevre but was never able to put the name to a face until now. Rochelle's law firm handled quite a few cases for the Le Fevres each year. The whole lot of them enjoyed suing people as a hobby.

"Oh, you poor thing," Rochelle told her. "I don't have the inconvenience of a bottomless bank account. However do you manage?"

But Grace didn't pick up on the sarcasm. "It's a burden, darling. It truly is. But listen. If you'll cooperate, I'll lend you my own makeup and wardrobe staff this evening. Oh no, no objections please. I'd consider it a favor. After all, this is a competition, and I want you looking your best when I win. I mean, what accomplishment is there in outshining something that doesn't shine in the first place?"

This incited a few snickers from the other contestants. Rochelle smiled. "All that glitters isn't gold, *darling*."

Grace scowled. "Have it your way, Rochelle, is it? But everyone here is a witness to my charitable offer. There will be no excuses when Grant votes you off in the very first Friendship Ceremony. And no excuses when a cab won't even pick you up to take you to the airport. They generally don't stop for tripe do they?"

As it turned out, Grace the Heiress was wrong; the sweatshirt Rochelle wore to dinner turned more heads than any gown ever could have. It may have had something to do with the fact that it was maroon with the acronym FSU in big bold golden font across the front—and that everyone had been made aware that Grant was a die-hard Gator fan. Or it could have been the fact that the collar had a permanent sweat ring from all the times she'd worked out in it. A better selection for their debut dinner just didn't exist.

Oh, Shelley and her supervisor Katya offered her every single dress in the wardrobe department that would fit and even offered to quickly tailor the ones that didn't, but Rochelle was having none of it. They were either too revealing, not revealing enough, too childish, too pornstar-ish, not pornstar-ish enough, or wouldn't go with the ratty ponytail she'd fashioned in her hair.

No, all of the sequined, tight-fitting dresses the wardrobe team had tried to fit her in seemed too…well, semi-formal.

Screw semi-formal. Grant didn't deserve semi-formal any more than Grace deserved to be bored with life because of her inheritance.

As she made her way to her seat, Rochelle could tell the cameramen were eating it up. She even took care to pound her tennis shoes against the tiled floors, reveling in the echo the shoes made in the cavernous dining room. One of the cameramen zoomed in on her smiling face, the other on Grant's scowling one. All the other women at the table wore dresses, which ranged from elegant to smutty (the twins), in colors from eggplant to princess pink (the twins). The one feature all the contestants shared was a shocked expression.

Except, of course, for Grace, who appeared quite annoyed.

Grant looked disgustingly handsome in his black suit and striking blue tie, both of which were accentuated by a sharply raised brow. After all these years, he had barely changed. Blond hair spiked and gelled into submission and green eyes that jumped out like a 3D movie. And obviously, Wardrobe had a difficult time finding him a suit that accommodated his broad shoulders; they strained against the fabric. Almost as much as he was straining to smile right now.

Elated with herself, Rochelle took the seat farthest from Grant, next to the Latina woman wearing a sumptuously fitted raspberry gown and creamy lipstick to match. "I'm Sonia," the beauty whispered to Rochelle, batting her long lashes. "And that's a pretty desperate attempt at attention."

Sonia gave her the once-over, at which Rochelle shrugged. The other woman quickly transitioned to a smile once she realized the cameras were filming their interaction. "But at least we all know you're educated," she said sweetly. "Good for you, pet."

Ha! Rochelle thought to herself. She wouldn't step foot on Florida State campus—University of Florida all the way, baby—but these girls didn't need to know that she only worked out in it to defile it with her sweat and stench. In fact, all these girls needed to know was that she was here for the cocktails. Once they realized she wasn't a threat–that she'd be voted off first–they'd all be besties. Maybe she'd even be voted Miss Congeniality. Or maybe that was beauty pageants she was thinking of…

"Thank you, Sonia. That's so kind of you to say. Did someone tell me you're a makeup artist? No wonder you look so exquisite this evening." Rochelle leaned aside so the waiter could pour her a glass of ice water. She placed a hand on his forearm and gave him what she hoped was an enticing smile. "Are you serving liquor this evening? I'm dying for a fireball whiskey."

The waiter, who was actually a looker himself, grinned. "I can make that happen."

Rochelle allowed herself a glance at Grant, whose jaw had grown tight. She gave him a beauty pageant wave—or her version of one. "Sorry to interrupt, Grant. You were saying something?"

"Actually, no," he said, eyes afire. "Not out loud, anyway."

A few giggles sprinkled from the other side of the table.

"Oh, do tell," said one of the twins. "You know, with all the time we'll be spending together, you won't be able to keep any secrets from us for long."

Grant gave her his signature Prince Charming smile, the one that used to make Rochelle swoon. Now it made her grind her teeth. He took Stephanie's hand—at least, Rochelle thought that twin was Stephanie—and placed a gentle kiss on it, lingering for a scandalous second. "There's a time and place for everything," he said adoringly.

Where in God's name is my whiskey? Is he really going to play this shallow game? With nine tramps, who only want him for his body and possibly money and the fame of being on the show to begin with?

Moron.

And where in God's name is my whiskey?

"So Grant, tell us about yourself," said Sakiya, the magnificent Asian woman who sat across the table. She'd had her hair entwined into a braided masterpiece atop her hair and Rochelle couldn't help being impressed. "Where did you go to college? What interests you? These are need-to-know things for us," Sakiya said. "How else are we expected to seduce you?"

Grant's smile didn't falter. "I graduated from the University of Florida. Any other Gators fans here?" He looked pointedly at Rochelle. And so did everyone else. Right then, the server presented her with two shots of whiskey. She took the opportunity to down the first, then the second, trying to look as unfeminine as possible. She wiped the excess from her mouth with the back of her hand, and then slammed the glass down on the table. A few gasps could be heard down the row of seats.

This could be all sorts of fun.

"And I'm a tactical training consultant," Grant continued, letting his gaze rest back on Sakiya. "Meaning, I can flip you on your back in seconds."

A tactical training consultant? That's what he'd been doing with his life? Whatever happened to his dream of becoming an aeronautical engineer? What exactly was a tactical training consultant, anyway?

And what do I care?

"Ohhh," said Grace. Why she was on a show like this was beyond Rochelle. Surely she couldn't be looking for true love. *Might as well be hunting Bigfoot.*

"Do you give private lessons?" Grace was saying.

"If you like." Then he smiled at her.

Rochelle allowed the waiter to pour her a glass of wine,

but she swirled it untouched and impotent, watching the contents almost reach the rim, willing it to actually spill so she could be excused. But it didn't. Deep within, the whiskey began to infuse heat throughout her body.

Grace gave Grant a demure smile. "When do we start?"

"Very soon, actually," he said. "But first, we have a contest."

"Like bingo?" the other twin—whose name might have been Cassie or Cassandra or something—said. She looked genuinely terrified. "I'm terrible at bingo."

Rochelle almost choked at the thought of anyone actually being terrible at bingo while Grant chuckled. "I'm going to give you a tour of the estate's gardens. And then we'll have a contest."

"But no bingo? Promise?"

Oh geez, Rochelle thought to herself. She was whiny *and* unadventurous. Definitely not Grant's type. *After he votes me off this week, she'll probably be next.*

Sonia didn't miss a beat. "Count me in."

Could someone's voice actually sound so naturally sultry? *Ew.*

All the others chortled at the mention of a contest. Rochelle could have upchucked onto the table. If only these girls knew what exactly they were competing for, what they were making fools of themselves for.

Then a smile spread across her face. *Speaking of acting foolish…* She dispatched with the wine in three big gulps. This earned her more appalled glances all around. If only she could bottle up arrogance and sell it to those faint of heart, she'd have been rich from harvesting this room alone.

Dinner, unfortunately, carried on smoothly. For the other contestants, anyway. For Rochelle, it proved to be an excellent opportunity to stuff her face, neglect her napkin and belch at every chance. Not to mention, ask for shots more often than was strictly ladylike. *God, but this sweatshirt is hot and stinky.*

And the new marinara stain on the S might retire it altogether. So sad.

After the dessert plates were removed — Rochelle had asked for seconds so everyone was waiting for her to finish — Grant stood. "So, ladies, it's been a pleasure dining with you. But now, onto the contest. Will you follow me, please?"

Rochelle remembered a time when Grant despised the spotlight, when he loathed being the center of attention. Which was unfortunate for him, because he turned female heads wherever he went. Now he seemed to languish in the spotlight like a fly on a pile of crap.

The twin Barbies flanked him on each side, latching onto his arms as if they were in danger of falling without his help, and accompanied him out the back French doors. Grudgingly, Rochelle followed the rest of the girls to the veranda. She was delighted to find that her gait was more of a stagger than anything else — and she was sure the shots of whiskey hadn't even caught up to her yet.

She felt a bit floaty as she accidentally glided into Maya, who had already stopped to listen to what Grant was babbling about at the head of the group. They walked off the veranda and into the grass. Maya, lovely as she was, gave Rochelle a disapproving look. "You're drunk," she whispered.

"Yeah," Rochelle giggled.

Under normal circumstances, she would have taken the time to appreciate the massive garden Grant showed them. There were benches, giant sculpted fountains, rows and beds of flowers everywhere. It was the type of place in which one could have taken up residence in a hammock, nurtured a good book, and hidden from the world. But in the dark, and under the influence, Rochelle decided to appreciate it another time. Another time when the cobblestone walkways didn't seem quite as uneven or the pathways quite so winding. And when Grant wasn't jabbering on and on about a stupid contest.

"Behind me, as you can see, ladies, is a maze made of hedges," Grant said. Rochelle definitely saw six-foot rows of hedges. A maze, though? *He's got to be kidding.* "There are a lot of dead ends. I hope you were paying attention to what I said at dinner, because I gave you clues about how to find your way out."

Oh crap. Maybe I shouldn't have hummed to myself every time he opened his mouth. Or called for more shots...

"What's the prize? A kiss maybe?" asked a perked-up Amber—that much Rochelle remembered from dinner, simply because she was a cookie-cutter big-breasted blonde. She looked like an Amber. Typical nightclub fare, as far as Rochelle was concerned. Completely not Grant's type.

But then again, Grant was being way more flirtatious than he ever had been ten years ago. And were his muscles bigger? She was pretty sure he hadn't been that shredded in college. Now that he'd taken off his suit jacket, it was obvious that his biceps and chest were threatening the seams of his shirt—and he wasn't even flexing.

Rochelle made a mental note to Google what a tactical training consultant actually was. It sounded violent and potentially brainless. Maybe Grant's total transformation into a dick was finalized during the time they'd spent apart.

"Better than a kiss," Grant said, grinning. *Maybe he was always a dick and I just didn't realize it.* That scenario sounded more legit. "Whoever finds their way out in the least amount of time gets to pick what we do on our first group date."

A rush of excited chatter circulated through the group. It cut off abruptly when Grant said, "Without further ado, I've selected Rochelle to go first."

Of course he has. This was probably payback for the nod to FSU. Or for dinner, in general.

Rochelle stumbled forward, thankful that she was wearing tennis shoes instead of the ground-piercing stilettos the other girls wore. And this sweatshirt? Perfect maze-maneuvering attire. Still, it was a bit stuffy, since they were in southern California in May, after all.

Oops. Did the ground just swerve or did I?

Grant reached out a hand just in time, catching Rochelle around the waist before she became better acquainted with the lawn. His grip felt strong, confident. He looked amused. Also, he smelled nice.

But why does he have four eyes? And why did he have to talk so fast? His words raced around her mind, her brain trying to grasp one or two of them, willing them to form actual sentences, but none of it made any sense. He said words like "attitude" and "agility" and "perseverance".

Is he giving me a pep talk? This mystery raged on in Rochelle's head even as he released her, turning her in the direction of some big-ass bushes; an opening in the row of hedges materialized in front of her. Oh, right. A maze or something. Her mom used to take her to corn mazes when she was younger. This was going to be easier than Amber after a few cocktails.

"Heh," she said to herself. "Easier than Amber."

Out of the corner of her eye, she saw Grant pinch his three noses.

"What?" she said. "What'd I say?"

He gave her a solid shove toward the entrance, and she helped by moving her feet in that direction, but the opening kept getting farther and farther away. The alcohol in her blood made her shoes feel as heavy as anvils as she approached the entryway, and it might have been the reason she advanced on it in a zigzag-like pattern.

Finally, she rounded the first corner and was greeted by a long corridor of more hedge. Deciding the best way to win was to run everywhere — the faster she found dead ends, the faster she could backtrack and find her way out — she picked up the pace and was proud when one foot obediently fell in front of the other. It wasn't exactly a straight line by any means, but at least she didn't fall. The bushes did hurt when she scraped against them, though; she might have been bleeding on her elbow from a corner mishap, though the pain was delayed and promptly numbed by the glory that was alcohol.

After a while, her initial momentum failed. She slowed to a walk, then a trudge. Each dead end looked exactly like the last; it was like getting assaulted by deja vu. Surely she wasn't walking in circles? *Of course not. I'm practically a professional.*

A few more minutes passed, and her aching head forced her to stop and take a break. She sat on the ground, drawing her knees to her chest. How nice it felt not to be careening back and forth between the hedge walls. Who knew traipsing in the bushes could make you so dizzy?

Overhead, the moon emitted a comforting glow of luminescence that seemed to dull her sense of urgency. Surely she'd gained enough headway in the maze for a well-deserved reprieve. As far as fight or flight went, neither seemed appealing at the moment. But the grass beneath her did. It felt like a cushy pillow, supple and inviting under her rear.

Is picking the first—and last—of my dates on the show really that important? At the moment, the only pressing matter to her was how stiff and unwieldy her legs felt, and how much more her bladder could actually take without bursting. She giggled to herself, visualizing a demure Amber stepping into a puddle of urine with open-toed shoes. The temptation to pull her pants down taunted her until she fell over, snickering her musings into the breezy night.

Oooh, the grass was so soft and plush. And she felt so weighted down, like gravity was a thousand times stronger in this part of the garden.

Surely they won't miss me if I close my eyes for a minute.

Chapter Six

Grant placed his palms flat on Richie's desk and stared down at the man whose fault this was. "You're going to let her act like that? She wore an FSU sweatshirt to a semi-formal dinner, for God's sake. Then she drank herself into a coma."

They'd had to send a search team to find her, since she didn't pass out where the hidden cameras could see her. If getting carried out of the maze even qualified as finishing, she came in last place at a whopping forty-five minutes and twelve seconds. Stephanie, one of the twins, won first place by finishing at nine minutes and eight seconds. She picked skydiving as their group date; Rochelle would be thrilled. She'd been terrified of heights since she fell out of her tree house when she'd been seven years old.

But this was her own fault. Hers, and Richie's.

Richie shrugged, fixing his voice into a faux, practiced innocence. "I've asked around about the sweatshirt and it turns out that she had a last-minute wardrobe malfunction. Don't worry though. It will be great for ratings. So will the drunken maze thing."

Grant crossed his arms. "Really? Because I asked around, too, and several of our lovely contestants said the 'wardrobe malfunction' was that she refused to put on any dress chosen for her. You realize why she wore a FSU shirt, don't you, Richie. I hate that team. And as for ratings, I don't give a rat's—"

"Please, lower your voice. This isn't as bad as it seems."

"She's disrespecting this show! She's disrespecting me. Why should I keep her around for that?"

Richie pressed his fingertips together thoughtfully. "This woman was the love of your life and you don't recognize what she's doing? I find that hard to believe."

"*You* said she was the love of my life. *I* told you I'd vote her off first chance."

But Richie only laughed. "I thought you'd be happy about this turn of events. About what it means for you."

Grant scowled. "Are you incapable of being direct?"

"Isn't it obvious, Grant? She's making what I would call a tremendous effort for you to vote her off. Which means she still has feelings for you."

"You have a warped sense of reasoning." She might have feelings for him, but they sure as hell weren't romantic in any way. What, she was trying to woo him with a sweatshirt that smelled like hot dumpster trash? Richie was crazy.

"She can't stand to be around you because of all the feelings it dredges up. Is that so hard to understand?"

Grant blinked. It actually wasn't; he could relate. He wished he could turn off the memories her presence provoked in him. "You can't let her run wild on the set, Richie. She's making a joke out of your show. Don't you care about that?"

Richie laughed. "She's doing exactly what I'd hoped she'd do. The question is, are you going to let her beat you at this game?"

Grant took the seat behind him and leaned on Richie's desk with his forearms. Of course she was trying to get voted off the show. She hated his guts and had an entire decade to let this medley of hatred and anger simmer. This was her loophole. Her way of getting out of the contract. "You don't know Chelle. She won't give up. These tantrums will only get worse."

"Look," Richie said with a sympathetic sigh that barely hid his delight. "There's a fine line between love and hate. Haven't you ever heard that? She obviously has strong feelings toward you."

Grant wiped a hand down his face. Changing Rochelle's mind about anything had always been a challenge. But changing her heart? Was that even possible? "Why would I care about her feelings?"

"I'm not sure exactly what your motives are. But if the woman has feelings, isn't it worth exploring for just a little while longer? If you don't like what comes of it, then by all means, vote her off. But aren't you a little curious to see what's become of Rochelle after all these years?"

As much as Grant knew Richie was selling him a line to get his way, he also knew he was a little curious to see the woman Rochelle had become. And maybe he'd give her the opportunity to see what *she'd* miss out on all these years.

"You handled yourself quite well last night," Richie

continued. "Very composed for the situation."

"Am I just supposed to ignore her behavior? That's not fair to the other women."

Richie smirked. "Do you even remember the names of any of the other women?"

Touché.

He hadn't so much as considered that any of the other contestants could be a match for him. All he could concentrate on was Rochelle. Even during dinner last night, when he'd been engaging in conversation with everyone but her, his attention had always slithered back in her direction. It infuriated him when she appeared to be flirting with the server.

It still infuriated him.

He should keep her here, just for that. He considered starting a list of all the reasons he should keep Rochelle on the show. After all, she had led him on all those years ago, made him believe that he mattered to her, that they had been more serious than the average college couple. He could let her suffer for a bit longer for that, couldn't he? And maybe, just maybe, this would give him some real closure. He wasn't over her. Maybe he could move on if she continued to act like this. Maybe he'd thank his lucky stars when she walked out on him again. "Sorry I wasted your time, Richie."

G rant sat on the edge of his bed and dialed Colby's number, putting the cell on speaker phone so he could finish tying his shoes. He wasn't supposed to have any contact with the outside world during filming, but he'd been able

to smuggle a phone in; he had to be able to check in on the
consultant business he and Colby shared. Colby took care of
the financial aspect, while Grant served as the talent.

His friend answered with a yawn. "You met the woman
of your dreams yet?"

"If you mean Rochelle Ransom, yes, I did happen to
have a run in with her."

"Rochelle Ran— You're kidding. Where did you see
her?"

"She's a contestant on the show," Grant said, sliding his
other shoe on. "And you're never going to believe what happened." After Grant explained everything to his best friend,
including his plans to get her back, or if not, hopefully get
some closure, Colby let out a long whistling breath.

"Dude, you're playing with fire. Maybe you should just
quit. It's not like I couldn't use you here. You and Rochelle
don't mix, remember?"

Grant resented that, even coming from Colby. His friend
knew how crazy he had been about Chelle. And he knew
why it had ended. So, to say they hadn't mixed, was like saying what they had wasn't real. For some reason he wasn't
okay with that, even if that's what Rochelle had thought.

Wow, overthinking it a bit?

"So what are you going to do?" Colby asked. "You could
just vote her off. Save you both the trouble."

"Actually, I was thinking of keeping her around for a
while." Of course, he couldn't tell his friend *why* he wanted
to keep her around. He wouldn't approve.

Colby sighed. "I don't want to see you hurt again, man.
That's all."

The last thing he needed was for Colby to get sentimental.

Besides, he was as far from getting hurt as a person could be. He was practically immune to Rochelle Ransom now. "Listen, I've got to go," he said, standing. "I've got filming in fifteen minutes. Everything okay on your end?"

He could almost hear Colby rolling his eyes. "Everything's fine, Grant. No one has died in your absence yet."

"Do me a favor and check in on Mrs. Windsor?" Mrs. Windsor was an elderly widow he'd trained in self-defense. He'd also set up a home security system for her before coming on the show. She'd had a very reasonable fear about some home invaders a few weeks ago since some of her neighbors had had their houses broken into. She was a prime target for that kind of thing and she knew it.

"Did that already. She's fine. A little feisty, actually."

Grant chuckled. "Knowledge is power."

Colby grew silent on the other end. Then he asked, "What was it like? Seeing her again, I mean."

Tortuous. Thrilling. Overwhelming. None of which he felt like divulging to Colby at the moment. "Surprising."

"If you don't want to talk about it, just say so."

"I don't want to talk about it." And then he hung up.

So far the Cozy Couch episode was as pleasant for Grant as dislocating his shoulder had been when he'd chased down a purse-snatcher in New York City. Of course, the initial getting-to-know you sessions were expected to be awkward, and Richie had warned him that in the past, contestants seemed to be the most nervous during this episode. Grant was, after all, interviewing the women one-on-one and if they didn't know how to answer, they could come off looking unintelligent, uninterested—or worse, according to Richie, boring.

In the beginning Grant was determined to put each contestant at ease. Now he was convinced *he* was the one who should have had a couple of drinks before filming. Shy was not a word that could be used to describe this particular group of contestants.

Especially not the one he just finished interviewing.

Grant watched as Sakiya—the artist he'd remember for saying weird things such as "drought of the soul"—exited the room. The only contestant he hadn't interviewed yet for the Cozy Couch Episode was Rochelle. No doubt a strategic play on Richie's part.

Out of the nine contestants so far, he did find a couple of them interesting. Maya for instance, stood out from the rest. Beautiful, compassionate, adventurous. She worked as a pediatric nurse during the day and lived life as a karaoke junkie at night. She was, by far, the most down to earth woman he'd ever met. He couldn't imagine that *she'd* ever have the kind of rage it took to slash someone's tires or key their dream Camaro.

And then there was Sonia, whose rollercoaster curves would normally have his hands itching to traverse them. A makeup artist and a self-proclaimed doomsday prepper, she was full of engaging conversation—he'd hardly gotten in a word—a fact which might be attributed to the reaction he had to her lips. As it turned out, keeping his eyes off her blood-orange lipstick wasn't as easy as he thought it'd be; he'd been wondering all along what Rochelle would look like wearing that color.

But there had been some crazies, too. Like Amber, the blonde fitness instructor who, in the middle of the interview, became bored and began to run in place. Or Grace, the Persian heiress who abruptly informed him that if they were to marry, he would have to convert to a religion she had recently developed herself. Something about being baptized in diamond water.

Or he could have nodded off and dreamt that part.

What he was sure about was this: the questions on his prompt card, the questions he was required to ask each contestant, were nothing close to what he wanted to know about Rochelle. Well, maybe the first one had some appeal: *Why did you choose to audition for Luring Love?*

That was one he'd been trying to figure out from the beginning. Hopefully, she'd answer honestly. Then again, maybe he didn't want to know. If she was looking for the man of her dreams, for instance, he'd be crushed. He could have been that man, if she'd given him that chance.

The door to the romantically decorated living room opened and in strolled Rochelle. She wore tight jeans that hugged her mouth-watering hips. Her halter top showed just a peek of his favorite breasts—which seemed to have gotten perkier since their last naked encounter. Or maybe it was just that she was showing more of them than she used to. Her hair cascaded around her face like she'd just experienced an exhilarating walk on a breezy beach—or a scream-worthy toss in the bed. That used to be his favorite look on her—hair down, walking barefoot around his dorm room wearing only her panties and one of his T-shirts.

It was that memory that left its mark on Grant. He closed his eyes against the sight of her now, hoping the camera didn't capture on his face what his body couldn't ignore—raw desire.

"Am I boring you already?" Rochelle said, taking the seat next to him.

"Never," he said. "Last but not least, right?"

"Don't get your hopes up."

He felt his nostrils flare. She planned to be rude again, like she had been at dinner last night. She was going to try to humiliate him all over again. And what kind of man would he come across as, if he took this sort of crap from her? It was out of the question. He would play her game. And he would win. "After your performance in the maze last night, how could my hopes possibly even hit knee high?"

"Cut!" someone yelled. It was Chris. He stalked up to them, amusement dancing in his eyes. "We can't mention the maze competition here, because this episode will air before that. So keep to small talk, okay? The witty stuff is good, though. Loving it."

Rochelle offered him a tight smile. "Will do."

"Perfect," Grant said, pleased with himself. Rochelle may have mastered the indifferent-attorney expression, but in her eyes flared a certain rage. Her lip twitched almost imperceptibly. "Thanks, Chris."

"Aaaand rolling!" Chris said, retaking the director's seat a few feet away.

Grant could practically feel the cameras focusing back on him. "I've decided to be America's reporter for the day," he said, having already memorized his lines. "So I have a few questions to ask that I think everyone will want to know—including me." Their eyes locked. So did Rochelle's jaw. Grant paused for effect. Then, "Why on earth would you choose to audition for a sleazy show like *Luring Love?*"

"CUT!" yelled Chris.

"I mean, have you *really* drained the dating pool already?" Grant continued, getting angrier with each word out of his mouth. These were, after all, valid questions. Never in a million years would Rochelle have chased after a man—so why the hell was she here? "What would your mother say? Coming on a show like this to paw at a man who's already got nine other women doing the same thing?"

"I said cut!" Chris growled.

"Oh, are we going to talk about mothers, then?" Rochelle flung back her hair. "Instead of dating pools, let's talk about *gene* pools—and the fact that you and your *four* siblings originated from separate ones!"

"Cut, cut, cut!" Chris had his hand on Grant's shoulder, but Grant wouldn't turn his eyes away from Rochelle. Her expression read *Challenge Accepted.*

Did she really just insult his mother's...need for variety in life? He couldn't let that low blow go unpunished. "Let's *do* talk about gene pools and how we both know that cleavage of *that* particular magnitude doesn't run in your family."

Taken aback, Rochelle clutched at her shirt. Grant felt a win on the horizon, if hurling mother insults could, in fact, be considered winning at anything. "It's a halter top, moron. It's *designed* for cleavage. Besides, you didn't seem to be complaining when I walked in!" she added.

His mouth fell ajar. *She noticed me noticing. Did the crew? Will America?* "It doesn't suit you," he blurted. A complete lie. It enhanced an already irresistible figure—so much so that he might have been willing to change his general opinion on how much cleavage a woman should expose in public. In fact, he suspected he'd change his view on world peace if Rochelle sat on his lap and asked him to.

"Really? Everything underneath suited the hell out of you before!"

"For God's sake," Chris said, standing in front of Grant to block his view of Rochelle. "Are we speaking the same language?"

But they just glared at each other.

"Hello? Anybody home?" Chris snapped in front of his face, once, twice. The third time Grant caught his wrist and applied enough pressure for the show's host to grimace. "Okay, okay," Chris said, snatching his arm away. "You realize we can't air any of that conversation, right? And that these little do-overs are costing the studio money?"

"So sorry, Christopher Schnartz-*Legend*," Rochelle said behind him. "Did you pick that name yourself? Because let me tell you something: You wish."

Chris turned to face her, and she flashed him a magnificent smile. "I was wondering when you were going to say something," he said. "As I recall, 'charming' was never something you could add to your college applications."

"And 'legend' was never a title you could claim in the bedroom, I hear. But good for you; you made it into Hollywood. As a reality TV show host, but still."

Chris's nostrils flared.

She smiled again. "Grant and I were just kidding with all the back and forth, weren't we, Grant? Just warming up to each other." She had the audacity to give Grant an encouraging look. A look that clearly implied he was the child in this incident.

Some things never changed.

"Warming up like a bomb, you mean," Chris muttered. There had been a time when Chris liked Rochelle, years ago. Grant wondered if that was going to change over the course of the show. "Fine." He looked at the crew, most of whom were stunned to silence. "Everything is fine. We're going to start over, okay everyone? From the beginning. In fact, Rochelle, could you just go back and make another entrance? I feel this scene is tainted somehow. Let's clear the air, shall we?" If Chris was still feeling bitter about his exchange with Rochelle, he certainly didn't show it. He was all business as usual. Maybe this was the right job for him after all.

"Of course, Chris," Rochelle said. "Anything you want. No more do-overs." Her voice was light and bubbly, devoid of the teeming venom she'd displayed not minutes before. A tigress transformed into a kitten, she stood demurely, and then strolled to the door in what Grant would call a woman-swagger.

And she never came back.

Chapter Seven

Even as the plane began its glide down the runway, Rochelle's stomach tied itself into about eighteen different knots of hysteria. The inside of the plane was hollow, with nylon straps tucked along each wall, and from it, an outreaching cord clamped to each person—a cord that each beautiful contestant would eventually discard in favor of jumping from the safety of this rickety flying metal heap someone, somehow, had deemed capable of flight.

The ride down the runway was bumpy and uncomfortable, and they sped along long enough for Rochelle to nurture a small hope that maybe the plane couldn't take off for some reason and they'd just have to cancel this idiotic group date. Oh, but no. When they finally lifted off the ground, Rochelle's knees visibly shook—something her instructor didn't miss, since he was strapped to her very intimately at the moment.

"You don't have to do this," he yelled in her ear. "Skydiving is not for everyone."

Like hell I don't. I'm not going to be the only contestant to chicken out. Never in a handful of millennium would I give Grant Drake the satisfaction of seeing me fail.

Skydiving shouldn't be for *anyone*, she wanted to inform the muscle-bound instructor, but he was definitely ex-military-drill-sergeant-ready to argue, and she wasn't in the mood for a dispute with a bull. Plus, she didn't want to start a conversation with him at all, given that his breath smelled like pickled toe fungus. Taking several breaths away from him—breaths that teetered on the verge of gulps—she felt herself calm down. Sort of.

Oh, wait. That's not calming down, that's just me attempting to voluntarily pass out.

She stared vehemently at the back of Stephanie's head, the twin who'd won the Garden Maze competition and got them all in this situation in the first place. She was the only one with no instructor strapped onto to her. She was also the only one who had done this countless times. *She's the one I'll strangle slowly with the chord of her own parachute once this is all over.* Even steel-nerved Maya looked apprehensive as she peered out of her window, down at the glorious land they had been walking around on just minutes before. Still, Maya tried to manage good-natured chitchat with her instructor, who seemed more than taken with her. And why wouldn't he be? Maya was dazzling, even in this hideous skydiving gear. The goggles actually looked cute on her.

At the back of the plane, Rochelle caught a glimpse of Grant a few victims down; he'd volunteered to be the first to jump, generous soul that he was. It was the sort of kindness he'd inherited from his mother. Rochelle nearly winced, just as she almost had earlier when she'd insulted his mother,

Sharon, in front of the cameras during the Cozy Couch session.

The truth was, that woman had been a Godsend to Rochelle in her younger years. It was just that Grant Drake knew what buttons to push. Even now, he was listening over his shoulder to what his instructor had to say, all the while giving Rochelle a look she knew well. He'd given her that look at college parties and at scary movies. It was the *Are you going to barf?* look. After their confrontation yesterday during the couch session, she wondered why he even cared. *Probably so he can stay upwind while I upchuck.*

She shrugged back at him in answer, even as her mouth watered.

Grant turned to his instructor and while Rochelle could hear them speaking, she couldn't make out the words. Grant's instructor unstrapped himself from him and made his way through the middle of jumpers, until he reached Rochelle. He put a hand behind her, presumably on her own instructor's shoulder. "We're calling this one," he said, nodding at Rochelle. "She's not up for it."

"What?" she shrieked. "No! I'm doing this. Period." *Oh my God.*

Grant's instructor gave her a doubtful look. "Some people can't handle heights. It's nothing to be ashamed of. Honey, your face is gray."

"Maybe I'm not a fan of heights, but I'm certainly not *afraid* of them," she said, turning her nose up with the lie. She suddenly remembered what it had felt like to fall head first from her rickety tree house when she'd been seven years old. *Who wouldn't be afraid of heights after head-butting the ground?*

Grant had made his way up to them. "Maybe you should go first," he said happily. "It's all the anticipation that's making you so nervous, I bet. Better to just get it over with."

"Excellent idea!" her instructor chimed in behind her.

Wait, what?

This seemed to interest Grant's instructor—whose name she thought was Harold. Harold gave her an admiring look. "Yes, let's do that then."

Oh. My. God.

"Tell you what," said Harold. "Make your way to the back of the plane now. We've reached optimal height.

When she opened her mouth to protest, Harold cut her off. "Don't worry, Grant won't mind. He was just going first as a courtesy anyhow."

Before she could think to fight, her instructor was using his hips to jar her forward, closer to the jump door. *Omigod, omigod, omigod.* On her way she got dirty looks from the other contestants. *They think I'm doing this for brownie points!*

But do I really care what they think? I'm jumping off a freaking plane!

"We're almost to the drop point," the guy attached at her hip said. With that, he opened the door separating life and death. The world below them appeared as clouds, the lakes as mere mud puddles, and the houses as specks, all separated by intersecting stretches of what Rochelle assumed were roads.

No, no, no.

The tree-house incident had broken her arm, given her a concussion and her whole body had been sore for days on end. The tree house had towered about six whole feet off the ground. How many thousands of feet away from precious earth were they now?

Surely, it would be a painless death. Maybe she could even find a way to land head first, so she'd be brained instantly.

"This is really brave of you to do," said the drill sergeant in her ear. "Now, on the count of three. One…Two…"

"Wait, wait! I—"

"Three!"

As they tilted out of the plane, she clutched the threshold of the door.

Rochelle opened her mouth to scream.

And vomited instead.

The sound of chunks making contact with the jumpers behind them was the last thing she remembered.

Chapter Eight

Grant waited in the lavish courtyard outside the mansion. The contestants were due any minute to arrive for the Friendship Ceremony. He'd have to decide which one would be the first to be voted off of *Luring Love*. That's when he'd hand the exiting woman a monstrous bouquet of fragrant sweet peas—a symbol of friendship.

And he knew exactly what he had to do.

Chelle didn't want to be here. She'd made that abundantly clear. Was it still the right choice to keep her here? Yes, yes it was. It was just too fun to get under her skin, the way he had on the plane. The way her face had grown pale, then a shade of green he'd never seen before. Maybe next time she'd think about wearing a smelly sweatshirt to dinner.

And there would be a next time. Voting Rochelle off now, just when things were starting to get entertaining, was out of the question. Richie had been right. He could play the game, too.

When the contestants began to appear, all sumptuously dressed and smiling, he adorned a serious face—per Richie's instructions—and waited for them to line up in front of him. Some appeared excited, some confident, and others nervous. Grant felt overwhelming relief when Rochelle showed up dressed for the occasion, wearing a long blue evening gown that enveloped her figure in all the appetizing places. She appeared neither excited nor confident nor nervous. If he had to pinpoint her mood, he'd guess it was somewhere in the vicinity of queasy. *At least she bothered to bathe tonight.* After their first dinner on air, he wouldn't have put it past her to show up in her flight gear, complete with barely-digested lunch still in her hair.

All the contestants who'd been subjected to Rochelle's puke bath in the plane had recovered quite nicely. Most of them had even helped move her limp body to the front of the plane when she'd passed out before jumping.

On Chris Legend's cue, Grant cleared his throat. He knew his cheesy lines well. He kicked off the evening with, "I hope you all enjoyed today's group date as much as I did—including the little surprises along the way." This earned him a few giggles from the entourage. Grant couldn't help but notice that Chelle stiffened. She didn't meet his eyes.

He arranged a grin on his face. "Today you all showed great courage in agreeing to go skydiving. I looked up the statistics, and less than one percent of the world's population is brave enough to do so. Bravo for you." *He would never in a million years say the word "bravo". Scripts were so forced sometimes.*

He walked down the line, continuing what he felt was a condescending speech. *Suspense, suspense, suspense,* he could hear Richie say. He was supposed to drag out the Friendship Ceremony for as long as possible. He was supposed to pause often, in case they edited that point for a commercial break. He was supposed to be enjoying himself. "I didn't realize how difficult the Friendship Ceremony was going to be for me. I mean, I've just met you all, and now I have to send one of you away. It feels so unfair." He paused and looked at Sakiya long enough for the camera to focus on her now apprehensive expression. This look meant nothing to him—it was just another cliff-hanging tactic, but the beautiful Asian woman seemed genuinely perplexed.

He hated himself for toying with her, but it had to be done in the name of tension. He tried to give her a reassuring smile, but she looked past him, tears welling in her eyes. *She was the artist*, he remembered. *The deep thinker. Who knew what she was thinking now?*

Grant moved on then, taking the hand of the next woman, who happened to be Jacquelyn, the blonde chef. She showed none of the anxiety Sakiya had. She greeted him with a toothy smile and even went so far as to plant a friendly kiss on his cheek. "I assure you," she said, with a small country twang, "None of us want to leave your side."

She acted sweet as molasses now, but Grant remembered when he'd been trying to maneuver Chelle to the front of the plane, Jacquelyn had refused to be anywhere near them, not wanting to get her hands dirty. *Strike one*, he thought, even as he smiled back at her. Selfishness had always been a turn-off for him.

Next in line was Ellie, the shy school teacher. She wore colored contacts to match her turquoise dress tonight, instead of her normal chic glasses. During the Cozy Couch episode, she'd admitted that she wanted lots of children—as long as it was with the right person. She also headed up the local cancer support chapter, which organized fundraising walks and drives to raise money for research. Sometimes though, it seemed like she spaced out during the conversation. She was definitely paying attention now, though.

Grant walked away from the line of assembled beauties, to the stone pedestal that held the massive bouquet of sweet peas. He picked them up slowly, giving the camera time to soak up the act, and to scan the faces of each contestant as he did so. He turned to face them again.

"I know every man in America is jealous of me at this moment," he said, walking toward the ladies again. "I know every man in America envies the fact that I get this rare choice. It's like choosing between fine gems. A task that's almost impossible." He stopped, smelling the bouquet. The group of women seemed to collectively shift from one high heel to the other. Grant felt the camera crew getting antsy behind him. *He* was even tired of hearing himself talk.

"Jacquelyn, step forward, please," he said finally. This time her smile wavered. "Jacquelyn, one thing I love is a generous spirit. I didn't see that with you today on the plane. To me, you acted like you were above helping one of the other contestants. I hope that's not the real you."

"I'm…I'm sorry…" she stuttered. He felt like stable dirt for pointing out a woman's flaw on national television. Why, why, why did he agree to do this stupid show?

"I hope to see a nicer side of you as the show progresses. You can step back now."

Relief washed over her features as she realized she wasn't the recipient of the bouquet. A few of the contestants around her proceeded to offer her congratulatory hugs.

After everyone settled down, Grant said, "Maya, step forward please?"

She did so, with the grace of a ballerina, but she kept biting her lip ever so slightly.

"Maya, you handled yourself well today. I appreciate the kindness and compassion you showed for your fellow contestants. This is a competition, true. But you let it go when it counted. For that, and many other reasons, I want you to stay on the show with me."

She gave him a brilliant smile, throwing her arms around him. "You scared me for a minute there," she whispered in his ear. She smelled nice, like an exotic flower on a humid southern day.

When she released him and strolled back to the line, Grant became instantly aware of Rochelle's eyes on him. With a quick glance, he ascertained that her brow was raised, the one she used to accidentally arch when she was flustered. *Is she jealous of Maya?*

If she was, that meant she had some sort of feeling for him, right? Should he take advantage of her envy and drive her crazy with it? The thought pleased him more than a little.

Still he needed more strategizing for this game they were playing, and it wasn't something he could do in the middle of the Friendship Ceremony. He needed to end this. It wasn't fair to the other women here, to keep them hanging on his every word and action. Screw the ratings. "Stephanie, please step forward."

As she did, a glowing smile spread across her face. "Yes, Grant?" she said prettily.

"Stephanie," he said, trying to sound as friendly as

possible. "I admire your sense of adventure. That was the first time I've been skydiving, and I assure you, it won't be my last."

"Isn't it exhilarating?" she breathed.

"It is," he agreed. "But for a group date, I'm not sure it was the right choice. It seemed to me that your motives were to put the others at a disadvantage, and while I know there will be game playing involved here on the show, I didn't appreciate how much your activity choice tested the other women. The goal is to stand out, of course. I'm just not sure you did that in the best way."

Stephanie's face fell dramatically. "Oh. I see."

"For that reason," he said, slowly handing her the sweet peas, "I'm saying goodbye to you tonight. I hope we can still be friends."

Chris Legend broke the awkward silence that followed by stepping into camera view and putting forth his best host voice. Grant wondered where he learned to talk with such a pleasant and endearing tone. Certainly not while he was talking trash on the football field back in the day. "All right, ladies," Chris said. "So we've gotten a glimpse at how our bachelor thinks now. For those who are staying, I would certainly take note. For Stephanie, this is farewell. You have one hour to collect your belongings and leave the mansion."

Stephanie's twin sister Cassandra threw her arms around her in a fierce embrace while the other women began to file back into the mansion in varying degrees of shock and elation. Only Chelle stayed behind.

Their eyes locked. Her glower was unmistakable. She had expected to be the one voted off. Rage emanated off her as she slowly made her way toward him, past the hugging twins. She didn't stop until her nose almost touched Grant's chin. Chris, who was standing nearby, instructed the crew to stop filming.

"This won't ever make it to air anyway," he muttered. Obviously Richie'd had a chat with him about their unique circumstances. Especially after the Cozy Couch session.

"You've made a wrong choice," Rochelle said in a low voice.

"Are you feeling better?" he whispered.

She turned on her heel and strode away, shoulders square. The twins gave her an evil look as she passed, and she casually flipped them the bird. He watched as she disappeared into the house, his decision made.

I'm coming for you, Rochelle Ransom.

Chapter Nine

Rochelle cursed under her breath as she assessed herself in the mirror. It was the stringiest bikini she'd ever worn. It left nothing to the imagination, revealing every flaw she had. Her hips were too wide. Her legs weren't nearly as toned as they should have been. And the top felt two sizes too small, the little triangles barely covering her nipples. She'd had to get a Brazilian just to wear the bottom properly, which dug so high up her butt cheeks, she feared she'd never get the fabric back out.

This was all Grant Drake's fault.

Yet, it was bittersweet.

It was his turn to choose a group date, and he chose to have them all participate in a charity festival—which benefited battered women. *Why would he choose that?* He knew it hit close to home for her; her father had abused her mother for years, even before she and Grant met in college. He understood how she felt about helping battered women find their voice–find safety. *Is he purposely doing this so I'll try to win the prize—a one-on-one session with him? And if so, why?*

Have I not made it clear that I hate the entirety of his guts?

She pulled on a white T-shirt and jeans. What reason did he have to keep her here? Was he trying to peel the scab off the wound in her heart? Was he really that cruel?

She shook her head, pulling on her shoes. At least she'd raise the money for this charity in a way that would throw it all back in his face. Each of the contestants was responsible for creating her own booth—the woman who raised the most funds got the coveted prize of a one-on-one date with Grant. She had to admit to herself that the other contestants had great ideas and she was pleased that they'd been so creative.

Sonia, a makeup artist, was going to paint faces for the kids and do makeovers for the adults. Cassandra, the remaining twin—a dolphin trainer, as it turned out—was having a local aquarium set up an underwater petting zoo. Amber, the fitness instructor, was going to hold a raffle for a dozen personal training sessions. Sakiya, the official resident artist, would be drawing caricatures, and Maya chose to open a karaoke booth. Even the school teacher—Rochelle couldn't quite remember her name—was going to make balloon animals for the kids.

Grace, the in-house Persian princess, couldn't be bothered with a booth but had grandly announced that she would be donating a large sum for the cause and visiting booths she thought were interesting.

Since Rochelle lacked all the talents of her fellow contestants—what, was she going to open a legal consultation booth and bore people to death?—she decided to keep it simple: she'd set up a kissing booth. She wasn't particularly good at kissing, either, but it required hardly any overhead costs and very little skill. And it wasn't like she was offering tongue or anything. Sure, her sense of self-worth expected more of her, but no one ever choked to death by swallowing their pride. Aside from the simplicity though, she liked the idea of turning Grant off; despite his signing up for this deplorable show, he *used* to dislike easy women. And what would be easier than paying for a kiss? It was practically glorified prostitution.

Rochelle smiled to herself as she made her way down the majestic staircase. Maya was the only one standing in the foyer; she must have stayed behind to wait for her. During her time at the mansion, Rochelle had found it was the small things, such as making Grant wait for her, that brought her pleasure even in this self-created hell she found herself in. She just wished it didn't affect the nice ones, like Maya. She even hoped that after the show, Maya would still want to be her friend.

Probably not, though, because if I have anything to do with it, this will get much, much worse.

"Oh, am I late again?" Rochelle feigned surprise.

Maya nodded. "Everyone's in the limo." She gave Rochelle the once-over. "Jeans? Did you change your mind about the kissing booth?"

"I'm wearing a bikini underneath."

Maya scrunched her face. She was just the sort of decent person who would be repulsed by a kissing booth, and Rochelle liked her even more for it. "Are you sure you don't want to change your mind? Grant might get the wrong idea about you kissing other men in front of him. He might see that as a rejection."

Precisely. For once, he could experience the feeling of rejection.

But Maya didn't need to be bothered with such details, so Rochelle merely shrugged, linking her arm with Maya's and escorting her out to the circular driveway where the SUV limo was parked and waiting for them. "Nah," she said. "It's my strategy to make him insane with jealousy." She really was getting good at these lies.

Maya sighed. "Okay. Well, it's not too late to change your mind."

Rochelle almost blushed. *What must she think of me?* She decided Maya was too nice for her own good. This was a competition, and rather than trying to get Rochelle voted off, Maya was trying to help her strategize to stay on. Rochelle would return in kind, but the prize for winning the show was Grant.

Grant, the unfeeling bastard.

What a horrible trophy to take away from this sleazy game they were playing.

Rochelle's booth was elementary, consisting only of an umbrella to keep her from burning in the sun, and a lawn chair for those moments between eager customers. And eager they'd been. Men of all ages and sizes and from all walks of life had kissed her. So many that she was tempted to squirt an entire bottle of hand sanitizer in her mouth. And God, a shower would have been nice, too. But at least all the customers had followed the rules, giving her only small pecks on the lips, and taking a photo with her here and there.

Sure, she got dirty looks from women passing by. A kissing booth was a kissing booth was a kissing booth. But the cause was worthy, she admitted begrudgingly, and the payoff, so far, had been huge. Besides, she was an attorney. Dirty looks came with the job. She could outwardly handle poisonous glares and acidic whispers behind her back, even as she withered inside from the humiliation.

Worthy cause, worthy cause, worthy cause.

She hadn't seen Grant all day, not since she announced in the limo what her booth would entail. He'd found it repugnant, she could tell.

In the distance, Grant approached with the camera crew in tow. He paused briefly at Sakiya's booth, and from the admiring look on his face, was complimenting her on her work. Just as Rochelle was about to mutter something under her breath, she got another customer, effectively ending her break and the self-loathing session that had ensued.

"Is the kissing booth still open?" her new patron asked.

She turned her attention to him. Handsome. Really handsome, and probably right around her own age. "Of course," she said, trying her hardest to sound enthusiastic. "But I'm expensive. It's five dollars per kiss."

He laughed. "That's a bargain." He handed her five ones, which she gave to her assigned assistant in charge of the money box. Out of the corner of her eye, she could see Grant and the camera crew stop. One of the camera guys hurried over to get in on the juicy footage about to go down at the infamous kissing booth. Rochelle fought off a cringe.

Grant was watching. He would see everything, so she had to make this good. The thing was, America would be watching her, too. And judging her. Could she ever recover from the shame she felt, even as she stepped toward the man?

Worthy cause, worthy cause, worthy cause.

"You can come closer if you want," she said to her customer. "I don't bite."

"Not even if I pay extra?"

Oh dear God.

When he stepped closer, she pulled him in by his shirt collar. She could practically feel Grant watching them, and she wondered how much attention he was paying. Could he see her desperation? The indignity she felt? The hatred she directed at him for forcing her to go to extremes like this? *That's right, Grant Drake. This is your fault.*

So watch this.

"Did you happen to notice the rules?" she asked out of habit.

"Read 'em twice."

"Good." She slowly pressed her lips against his, and instead of a peck, she let them linger a bit. But when he opened his mouth for more, she stopped, pulling away. Lingering was one thing. Making out with a stranger on camera was quite another.

Her handsome customer stepped back in slight awe. "I could do that all day," he said, reaching for his wallet again.

"You'll have to get back in line," a voice called from beside them.

They turned to Grant, who strode toward them like a predator stalking its next meal. Rochelle's stomach somersaulted. She'd seen that look in his eye before.

She was in loads of trouble now.

Rochelle's dapper customer stepped away, allowing Grant room between them. Grant smiled at the man. "Rules are rules," he said, tilting his head toward the board in front of them. "Number three says you get one kiss, then have to go back to the end of the line."

The man nodded good-naturedly. "I'd wait in line all day for another kiss like that."

Grant's smile faltered, something Rochelle relished for the second it lasted. Recovering, Grant nodded toward the back of the line, which kept growing and growing, probably because of the camera crew now parked beside them. "If you don't hurry, it just might be all day."

To the older man in overalls next up in line, Grant extended his hand for a friendly shake. His one moment of resentment seemed to have dissipated in the summer breeze, and Rochelle couldn't help but feel disappointed at how short lived her victory had been. She did notice though, that Grant's eyes were still sharp, still steely. Was he jealous? And—did she care?

"Hi, my name is Grant Drake. These guys here are filming a show called *Luring Love*. Have you heard of it?"

The man scratched his white beard, a grimace puckering his expression. "I'm Magnus. Yeah, heard of it. My wife makes me watch it. Too political, if you ask me."

"Well, I can see why you'd think that. Listen, I'm this year's bachelor. Rochelle here is one of the contestants on the show. She chose to run a kissing booth to raise money for battered women. What do you think about that, Magnus?"

Her patron looked pointedly at her. "Well now, on the one hand, she seems to be raking in some dough for the charity. On the other…Well, you ought to open your eyes, son. My wife would call this strategizing. This young lady is trying to make you jealous by kissing a bunch of other fellas."

Grant laughed. Rochelle felt if her eyes got any wider, her eyeballs would fall out and bounce on the asphalt beneath them. *What is he doing?*

"You think so?" Grant was saying.

"It's plain as high noon, boy."

"Hmmm," Grant said thoughtfully. He studied Rochelle, his eyes locking with hers. "What do you think I should do about it, Magnus? Should I act jealous or pretend it doesn't bother me?"

Magnus shoved his hands in his overalls and rocked back on his heels. "I can't rightly say."

Grant nodded. "It's a tough call, isn't it?" He sighed. "Well, we've got to film me visiting Rochelle's booth, so if you don't mind, could I possibly cut in front of you? I hate to ask, but the crew's tired and ready for their break and this is the last shoot of the day."

"Aw heck, go ahead," says Magnus, waving his hand.

"Thanks, Magnus. You're a good sport." Grant turned to Rochelle then, his eyes flinty. He pulled out his wallet slowly, deliberately. "Who takes the money here?" he said without looking away from her.

Rochelle's assistant perked up behind them. "Um. I do, sir."

He offered her the briefest of smiles. "Good." From his wallet he retrieved some bills and handed it to her. "For my turn," he explained.

Without further warning, he grabbed Rochelle and

jerked her to him, using his hand to press her lower back into him. There was no space between them at all—except at their lips. Instantly, she regretted wearing the tiniest bikini on the planet. She might as well have been naked.

"I've paid for this fair and square," he told her softly.

"There are rules—" she choked out. Oh dear God, she was going to have to kiss Grant Drake. She wanted to fight, she did. She brought her hands to his chest, intending to push him away, but they stayed there, reveling in the feel of him beneath his shirt, in the new contours and the old. Her body seemed to melt into his, the way it always used to. She gritted her teeth against the reality of the situation. She was in Grant's arms again. And she was going to have to bear it.

Seeming to sense her urge to fight, he shook his head. "I've paid for this moment with more than money." And his mouth crushed down on hers. She tried to pull away, the rules and the money and the show be damned, but his prying tongue distracted her, flitting across her lips, asking for— then demanding—permission to enter. All she could think was to keep her mouth shut, to not allow him access, but he persevered, opening her wide. It was the kind of possessive kiss she used to love. It set every part of her on fire. One of his hands found the nape of her neck and pressed her closer still, the other cupped her hip, toying with the string holding everything together there, threatening to drive her mad. With his mouth, he opened her again and again with a kind of need she felt herself. With a kind of need she had never wanted to feel again.

At least, not with Grant Drake.

He lifted her from the ground to get better leverage, and all at once, a surge of applause resounded from around them.

The crowd was cheering them on, clapping and whistling as if they were at a rodeo instead of a kissing booth. No, they were cheering *him* on. Grant was in complete control of this situation. And she wasn't about to let that continue. If he wanted a kiss, she would give him one. Wrapping one of her legs around his thigh, she clutched him, clinging to him in a way that might not have been suitable for the viewers at home. This was, supposedly, a family show after all. She allowed herself an ample handful of his taut rear. They could edit that out if they wanted, as long as they captured his reaction to it.

He groaned into her lips, grinding himself against her bikini bottoms. "My God," he breathed against her mouth.

And that was when she stopped it. She had won. But in a way, he had won, too. She'd promised herself that Grant would never get to kiss her like that anymore. He didn't get to kiss her like this ever again. Yet there she was, attached to him like Velcro to carpet, drawing memories and feelings and pain to the surface. Not to mention something else she never expected, never dreamed she would feel again for him.

Desire.

Abruptly, she shoved him away, so hard that he stumbled a bit before catching his footing. For several long moments, she struggled to catch her breath, taking small satisfaction in the fact that he was doing the same. The roar of their small festival audience had heightened to a deafening clamor. In her panic, she'd almost forgotten about them. About the crew. About America.

Omigod.

Mortification settled over her as she looked at the camera, which was still focused directly on her face. Heat burned her swollen lips and seared her cheeks and seemed to spread like lava down her body. "Cut!" she screamed. "Cut!"

Chris Legend wriggled his way to the front of the crew. "That's a wrap," he said, visibly amused.

"That is *not* going on air," Rochelle informed him.

"Oh, yes, it is," Chris said. "It's the juiciest footage we've gotten all day."

She lunged then, but Grant caught her before she was able to get her hands around Chris's neck. Still, the show host looked a bit pale. Good—it was smart for him to acknowledge the very real danger he was almost in.

"We both agreed to this," Grant whispered in her ear, holding her in an impenetrable bear hug. *Since when did he get so strong?* "We both agreed that we'd play this game."

"We don't have to play this game," she hissed. Slowly, he let her slide down the length of him. "You could just vote me off."

He laughed, a loud, cruel sound that startled the people around him. "Not in a million years."

Chapter Ten

Tonight's Friendship Ceremony would be easy for Grant. There would be no more back and forth about whether or not he should let Rochelle off the hook, whether or not he should hand her the bouquet of sweet peas and let her be on her conniving way.

The kiss this afternoon at the festival changed everything. He would never let her go again. Not ever.

Even though she showed up to tonight's ceremony wearing hideous flannel pajamas and wet hair. Even though she gave him the death glare during his monologue for the sake of building tension on camera. Even though she faked a coughing attack in the middle of the take in a blatant attempt to be excused.

They still had something. There was still something that happened when their lips touched. Nothing as cheesy as a jolt or a spark. No, it was deeper than that, always had been. It was a craving, long-denied. An insatiable yearning, a hole that could never be filled no matter how long he was in possession of her mouth. Or everything else.

Tonight Grant was in no mood to string along his other victims. One by one, he pulled forward each contestant and told them plainly what they did or didn't do to please him that day. No pausing, no breaking, no hesitation, though most of it was commendation, anyway—even for Rochelle, whose kissing booth had managed to get under his skin better than any ambitious tick ever could. Watching her kiss other men… His jaw still hurt from clenching it so hard.

It was something he never wanted to see again.

At least tonight's choice was an easy one. Of all the contestants and their innovative ways to make money for the charity, one stood out like a rock among diamonds. "Grace, please step forward," he said amiably. This would be easy for him. The only hard part would be fixing his expression to show something other than disgust.

It was probably the first time the heiress had ever done what she was asked without question. Since the beginning, she'd refused to allow the studio's makeup artists to touch her, insisting on bringing in her own staff. She'd insisted on boarding the skydiving plane first. She'd turned down every selection of wine her server offered her at dinner, declaring it all inferior. Even the crew had taken to calling her Your Grace.

Smiling, Grant accepted her hand and placed a small kiss on it, which pleased her immensely, he could tell.

"Grace, your monetary donation today was very generous and greatly appreciated. It couldn't have gone to a better cause. But…" He paused for the camera, but mostly to keep Grace herself in suspense, rubbing her white-gloved hand with his thumb. "I like a woman who's not afraid to work. Who's willing to get dirty for a good cause. I have my wealth now, but what if I lose it all one day? What if you do? Would you be willing to work to put food on the table? Gas in the car? Keep the lights on? I know I would be willing to, and I expect the same from any woman I marry. Today, I saw that you aren't a team player." He walked to the pedestal and extracted the bouquet of sweet peas from it, fighting the urge to grin. "I'm afraid to say, I'd rather be friends than anything else."

"Wait," Grace said, stricken. "You're voting *me* off? Are you stupid? Look at this riffraff behind me! And it's *me* you're sending home?" She turned to Chris. "*Do* something."

One of the cameras followed the host as he walked onto the veranda where Grace and Grant stand. "I'm afraid there's nothing I can do," he said. "It's up to Grant to decide who stays and who goes. My condolences."

Chris was eating this up, Grant could tell. It was just the kind of outburst the show needed. Richie would practically drool when he saw this clip. It was amusing, after all, to see someone as poised as Your Grace looking as harassed as an agitated cat.

"You can keep your condolences," Grace spat. She turned to Grant. "You're nothing. What, I'm supposed to be *impressed* by your big biceps and dimples and the fact that you've built your own fortune? You built your fortune off of people like me. If people like me didn't need professional protection, people like you would be out of a job!"

Grant nodded. "You're right. If you people weren't so helpless, I'd be out on the street. Chris, remind me to send her a thank you card?"

Chris's eyes went wide. "Uh, will do, Grant."

This elicited chuckles from the crew behind him. Grace's nostrils flared. She snatched the bouquet from his hands and threw it to the ground, stomping on it as best she could in those daredevil stilettos of hers.

"That's not very nice," Grant observed.

"No," Chris said, thawing in time to enjoy the moment. "Not at all."

"Screw you both! Screw this show!" Grace stormed off like a frilly tornado of black tulle.

G rant could hear Colby shuffling papers on the other end of the phone. That was Colby, a diligent, multitasking fool. Grant knew he was lucky to have someone as trustworthy as him as his business partner. They'd met in college when he had been tutoring Colby in biology; Colby had been on scholarship for an accounting degree, and Grant was volunteering for his fraternity house. They'd hit it off immediately and had remained friends ever since.

"We've got a Mr. Ely Jameson practically banging down our door for you to train him in abduction prevention," Colby was saying. "Apparently he just won the Connecticut lottery and only now realized that the people he called friends, aren't."

He could tell his friend was only half-listening to him recount the events of the Friendship Ceremony. If he was going to snap his friend out of work mode, he had to do something drastic. He needed someone to talk to. He hoped being around all these women wasn't making him soft. "I kissed Rochelle," he blurted.

The paper shuffling stopped. Colby sucked in a breath. "What?"

Grant nodded into the phone, knowing the action was lost on his friend. "Rochelle opened a kissing booth for the charity fundraiser. So, I decided to help her out and—"

"Did she kiss you back?"

What kind of questions was that? "Of course she did."

Nothing. It was a rare thing for his business partner to be shocked into silence. "Well. That's…interesting."

Interesting? That's all he had to say? "I'm going after her. I want her back."

"And how does she feel about that?"

"She's elated. She doesn't just realize it yet."

More silence. It was the first time he'd ever considered Colby a useless confidante. "What's with you?" he said. "You thought *Luring Love* was a great idea when Chris pitched it to us. Now that I'm actually giving it a fair shot, you're about as excited as roadkill."

"Man, I'm sorry. It's just that…Well, is this what you really want? She destroyed you last time." Grant thought he could hear the clicking sound of a calculator.

"I took matters into my own hands. And anyway, she acted like she was destroyed, too, if keying my car was any indication." Of course she'd keyed his car. He'd callously broken up with her out of nowhere. She was destroyed. But he could change things now. Make them better. He knew it.

A long pause on the other end let Grant know he wasn't getting any help from Colby today. Maybe the guy just needed time for the shock to wear off. Then he'd be Grant's willing accomplice again. He always was. "I'll have to call you back. Richie will send someone looking for me if I don't show, and I can't risk getting busted on the phone."

"Okay. Keep me posted."

G rant opened the door to Richie's office and strolled in with a wary smile. Richie was waiting for him, sitting on the edge of his huge desk, a sheet of paper in his hands.

"You asked to see me, Richie?" Grant said.

The older man nodded. "Have a seat, Grant. Can I get you anything? Whiskey? Port? They stock this place with some amazing stuff."

"Are we celebrating?"

Richie grinned. It was an ugly grin. "I just got the ratings for the first episode." He shook the paper in his hand triumphantly. "Highest ratings since we've aired. In a word? Marvelous." He hopped down and walked around to sit in his high-backed chair. "You should hear what the target audience is saying about Rochelle. They cannot believe you didn't vote her off after the dinner stunt. And then the maze? Fans of the show are practically rioting!"

"Is rioting good?" Grant said. The actual filming of the show was ahead by a few weeks, so the first episode just aired last night. Grant didn't care to watch it. Living it was enough.

"Rioting is fantastic. Someone even started a blog called *Bachelor and the Beast* in order to get Rochelle voted off. They're reaching out to you, Grant. They want to help you. They're connecting with you in a way that's never happened before." When Grant said nothing, Richie gave him a thoughtful look. "How are things with Rochelle, anyway?"

"With Chelle, it's hard to say."

Richie gleefully slapped the desk. "Chris showed me the footage of the kissing booth. That was hot stuff! She really opened that door for you, didn't she?"

And for about a hundred other men, which still had him clenching his fists. But none of them received even a fraction of their money's worth. Not like he did.

"Chris said you paid her five hundred dollars. Was it worth it?"

Was making sure she won the booth competition—and therefore a one-on-one date with him—worth five hundred dollars? Of course it was. "She's always been a good kisser."

"I'll bet."

"So you called me here to tell me about the ratings?" Grant asked, bored already. Besides, he still had to go oversee the gym setup for the next group date. He was going to be teaching the contestants self-defense. He was hoping it would send a message to Rochelle. After all, she was the reason he'd started teaching self-defense in the first place. She and her mother had had a hard life living with Roy Ransom. If they had known self-defense, maybe they wouldn't have been his favorite targets.

"No, no. That's a bonus. Actually, I wanted to let you know that Rochelle came to me earlier today. Said she's not sure she can do this. She seemed really upset."

"Upset?"

"Upset in a good way."

Grant couldn't imagine a good kind of upset.

Richie shook his head. "Don't you see? Before, she was virtually an ice queen. You're defrosting her, Grant. She's coming around. I saw that kiss. Maybe you two are compatible after all?"

He wasn't sure if Richie really did see something in the kiss or if he was BS-ing. But what Grant *felt* during the kiss was very convincing. Rochelle was definitely coming around, even if it was against her will. There was a moment, a few sweet seconds, where she was Chelle again, and she was kissing him just as much as he was her. In fact, she'd tried to take over, and he'd allowed it, to his detriment, no less. It had left him with an appetite for her that kept him awake all night. "How did you talk her into staying this time?"

Richie winked. "Now Grant, that's an invasion of Rochelle's privacy, don't you think? How would you like it if I told her everything you and I talked about?"

"Point taken."

"So what's your strategy now?"

"Rochelle is too unpredictable for a strategy. The only thing I can do is plan for the unexpected."

"Good luck, my friend. And keep up the excellent work."

Chapter Eleven

Rochelle couldn't help but feel that she was in an endless beauty pageant where all the contestants were lined up on stage for inspection for days on end, expected to present themselves with an unwavering smile and sucked-in gut. Today, that stage was the gym of the mansion. All the treadmills, weights, and ellipticals had been removed, giving them a full view of themselves at every angle since the walls were floor-to-ceiling mirrors.

They were told to wear workout attire for today's group date, and Rochelle was more than happy to don her noxious anti-Grant team sweatshirt again, even though it meant technically complying with the show's expectations—something she'd grown too comfortable with doing, lately. She had to step up her game if she was going to get Grant to kick her off.

At this point though, she was unsure as to whether Richie wanted her to comply with the rules or not. He seemed excessively amused by the fact that she kept undermining the episodes in one way or the other—and she couldn't decide if she wanted the producer excessively amused or excessively irritated. All she really wanted was to be voted off the show. Especially after that kiss with Grant a few days ago.

Oh, the emotions it brought back. Feelings she'd long since packed down, poured concrete over, chained, and left to die in the deepest chambers of her heart. How could one kiss unearth the many feelings she'd worked so hard to entomb?

That can never happen again.

She was already planning her one-on-one date with Grant that she'd earned by having the highest-earning booth. She'd been irate to find that he'd paid not *five* dollars for the kiss, but *five hundred dollars*. That one kiss had brought in more money than any of the other booths had made all day. He'd basically rigged the competition with that stunt, just to get under her skin. Why else would he want a one-on-one date with her? Still, it was five hundred dollars toward helping battered women. Wasn't it worth the gaping crack in the armor she'd put on for this contest? Couldn't she pull herself together for that reason alone?

Of course she could.

Rochelle glanced around her now, using the mirrors to spy on the contestants not close to her in line. Maya was decently attired in an athletic T-shirt that somewhat hugged her, and plain black yoga pants. She couldn't hide her rock solid body even if she borrowed Rochelle's raunchy sweatshirt. Everyone else seemed to have taken the prompt to mean "wear the least possible while working out" or "if we can tell you're not wearing panties, you're doing it right" or "nothing is better than something".

They had yet to see Grant, but Chris Legend informed them that he was in the building and likely in makeup. Rochelle wondered how well he was adjusting to some good old-fashioned makeup. She hadn't detected anything ridiculous on him like eyeliner or lip gloss, but she could tell his complexion had a touch up, and there was no way he'd voluntarily stay clean shaven for this many straight days in a row. Not the old Grant, anyway.

Rochelle wondered why they had to keep waiting for Grant to arrive from his secret location anyway. Why couldn't he just stay in the mansion? Why did they bother separating the sultan from his harem?

The reasons weren't entirely obvious to Rochelle, especially if Richie wanted ratings. As the "season" progressed, Grant would eventually be permitted to stay the night with the contestants of his choice in the Paradise Suite—so why hold off the inevitable? It would have been way more convenient if they sped that particular segment along. Surely some of these girls had talents that would better sway Grant to vote Rochelle and her unworldly knowledge right off the show.

Because she sure as heck wasn't staying with him in the Paradise Suite.

Grant materialized at the door then as if she'd thought him into existence, and Rochelle found herself relieved to tuck away the insanity that the thought of spending a night in "paradise" with Grant could cause her. She also wondered if the Paradise Suite at least had a kitchenette, where knives would be readily available.

Confidently, Grant strode to the center of the room, giving the cameras time to focus on his face as he smiled and the contestants time to eat up his masculine gait. He was rather good at this whole reality show thing, Rochelle realized. But then again, what *wasn't* Grant good at?

Well, tact isn't his specialty.

"Ladies, how are you this morning?" Grant's generic little icebreaker was effective. Rigid stances melted into puddle-like, flirtatious statures and mindless fidgeting down the line. When his gaze met Rochelle's it had a deviousness to it that bothered her. Or rather, got her hot and bothered. Obviously satisfied with this result, he folded his hands in front of him and addressed all of them. "A few days ago, we participated in a festival, the proceeds of which went to care for victims of domestic abuse. I hope that gives you at least a small glance into my character and my beliefs. Today, I want to show you even more."

He walked down the line then, as if he was an officer addressing a row of soldiers. "The festival had its purpose; there will always be victims of domestic violence. There will always be someone who needs our help. But today I want to concentrate on prevention. As you all know, I'm a tactical training consultant. Which means, among other things, I teach people how to defend themselves. For today's group date, I will show you, one-on-one, how to defend yourself during an attack."

Excitement bubbled forth from the line while Rochelle choked back an emotion she couldn't quite name. Her mother had been the victim of her father's abuse for their whole marriage. It was one thing Rochelle could not, and never had been able to, tolerate. That Grant was so interested in being an advocate for such a cause… Did it have something to do with her, with her past? Or was he mocking her?

Back when they were still together, he'd known how important it was to her that abused women had a voice. He understood what she went through as a child. In college, he'd helped her pass out flyers to raise awareness, to get his frat brothers to hold fundraisers for domestic abuse shelters. And the warmth and strength of his embrace had always been there when Rochelle herself broke down on occasion. When *she* needed to cry about the injustice of it all. He had been there for all of it.

First the festival, and now this. Was he *trying* to revive horrible memories of her childhood? Or was he *trying* to stroke her nerves like some sort of stringed instrument, reminding her of everything she'd lost when she walked out of his life forever? His love, his compassion, his warmth. Did he still care about those things? Did he still care about *her*?

No, she had to stop that line of thinking. She reminded herself that she didn't lose everything. Because she'd never had it. None of it had been real. If any of it had been real, he wouldn't have broken up with her and definitely not as callously as he did. She had been prepared to move in with him, to ask him to come with her. To take the next step in life with her.

But he pummeled it all with his words. *I don't think we're working out. I've grown bored with you, in fact. So I guess this whole law school thing worked out for the best.* He'd been so cold, so indifferent, even when congratulating her.

Rochelle swallowed bile back down into her churning gut. She couldn't let him do this to her. Not again. She had to get out of here.

"Who would like to go first?" Grant was saying. Of course, everyone save Rochelle raised their hand, even Maya. Rochelle couldn't help but feel a small betrayal that Maya was showing genuine interest in Grant. *Of course she is, stupid. That's the reason she came on this show. Not everyone ditches their life and lucrative career to participate on a deplorable show to champion a sinking cause.*

Some people were actually looking for love.

Oh, Maya. Don't try to win this. Don't try to win him. You deserve so much better.

An overwhelming sense of disgust engulfed her. This was just a chance for him to put his hands all over these willing, enchanted nitwits under the guise of a good cause—*her* good cause. It was though he was slapping her in the face. She knew the drill. She'd taken many a self-defense class herself. Even taught one at Helping Hands. The intimacy between trainer and trainee could be invasive, if done unprofessionally. And this? This had all the makings of a petting zoo. Grant would probably grope each and every one of them in the name of teaching self-defense.

He's not going to turn something I care about into a joke.

"I'll go first," Rochelle said, stepping forward so she was the most visible in line. Why Grant looked so surprised she couldn't possibly have guessed. He'd been the perfect sidekick in college. The perfect helper. He, of all people, would know how she felt about this group date. Of *course* she would be interested in self-defense. Of *course* she would be interested in helping to prevent the abuse of victims. Statistically, they both knew that at least two of the women here could already have been victims themselves. Or had he forgotten even the most basic parts of their relationship? Had she really been so blind to his insensitivity? Apparently so. He'd taken something she had been passionate about and exploited it for a living, after all.

"Rochelle, you can be my first student," Grant said. She wanted to strangle him for looking so pleased.

Careful to arrange her expression into one of curiosity and uncertainty, she approached him slowly. "Is this going to hurt?" she asked good-naturedly. Of course it was going to hurt. It just wasn't going to hurt *her*.

His smile wavered. "I would never hurt you."

The flame of temper licked her insides. *I would never hurt you.* Words they both knew were not true.

She stood in front him, and they exchanged a look. His was quizzical, she decided. *Why the sudden cooperation?* he asked with his eyes.

Because of this, she answered with a small smile.

And she promptly kneed him in the groin as hard as she could.

Chapter Twelve

Grant groaned, carefully pulling the ice pack from the crotch of his boxers and placing it on the nightstand beside his bed. If he left it on any longer, his testicles would have been two ice cubes clinking around in his pants. Besides, the limo would be there in half an hour to pick him up and take him to the Friendship Ceremony, and though he still couldn't move without feeling his last meal slide up his throat, he was determined to show up and exercise his right to eliminate a woman he'd never marry.

Forget Rochelle.

Forget her distracting smile and her bony knee and her accurate aim. Forget her false concern as he fell to the gym floor. Forget her innocent expression as she chattered worriedly with the other contestants while the medics fell upon him, ascertaining that his balls were, in fact, still intact. It had been *her* voice he'd heard over everyone else. *Her* voice that he couldn't drown out even over the scurry of the camera crew trying to get ratings-worthy shots of his agony. "I thought he would protect himself," she'd protested. "It's the oldest trick in the book," she'd added. "I thought for sure he would see that coming. He did say he was an expert, didn't he?" she'd asked.

"Well, you were probably supposed to wait for his instruction," someone had argued. Amber, maybe?

"Yeah, like, for him to count to three or something," another had said.

"But he didn't tell us that," Rochelle maintained. "I thought I was supposed to be fighting for my life." Between the hoard of people surrounding him, Grant could see her biting her bottom lip, looking horrified to the untrained eye. But none of it reconciled with the victory that had been swarming in her gaze.

"I'm sure everything will be okay." That had been Maya in her soothing nurse's voice. "He'll just need a few days of rest."

"Oh no," said Sonia, her sophisticated Hispanic accent dripping with counterfeit sympathy. "That means the one-on-one date you won at the festival will have to be postponed, Rochelle. You really screwed yourself there." And then she gave a small laugh, as if Rochelle were an idiot.

As if Rochelle Ransom hadn't just achieved exactly what she'd hoped for.

So, now he had more proof that she wasn't above humiliating him on camera. Only she'd graduated to inflicting physical pain instead of just playing incessant mind games. Was there anything she *wouldn't* do to get eliminated from the show? What *else* should he be prepared to endure? And was it worth it?

His mind kept wandering back to their kiss at the festival—to the few seconds they'd shared where they were alone, just Grant and Chelle, kissing because that was the most natural thing in the world for the two of them. He thought of the way she'd kissed him back. The way she pressed herself into him, without letting the past poison the moment. The way she'd become Chelle again, and not some vicious beast with obvious disregard for the health of their future children together.

Was there anything he wouldn't endure to have *that* Chelle back again? To have her in his arms, in his bed, in his life?

He couldn't think of a single thing he'd let get in the way of having her, despite what he'd learned of the woman she'd become. He snorted. Maybe another kick to the balls would actually do him good. Because right now, he was still a pathetic, irrationally lovesick puppy who would probably follow her anywhere.

But that didn't mean he couldn't protect himself from her. She was bent on making war; at the very least he needed to be on the offensive until she simmered down. With that thought in mind, he gently pulled on his slacks and slid on his button up shirt in preparation for the evening's Friendship Ceremony.

The women were all lined up and waiting for him by the time he arrived at the mansion. Walking with slow, deliberate movements in order not to jostle his swollen testes, he made his way to his position for filming on the veranda. Nearby, the bouquet of sweet peas sat on a short stone pedestal, and it was this, rather than Grant, that the contestants seemed to focus on.

Chris Legend gave him a welcoming slap on the back, which made Grant grit his teeth.

"Still feeling tender?" Chris said.

"A bit," Grant answered, glaring at Rochelle. She was oblivious though, chatting happily with Maya who, for her part, kept throwing concerned glances at Grant. Glances with questions in them. *She wants to know if I'm okay. Why can't I be chasing after a woman like that?*

"A lesser man wouldn't have survived. You're a good sport to shoot the ceremony tonight. Richie said we could give you a day or two to rest."

"Thanks for your concern, but I'm fine."

Chris leaned in. "I hope this little, uh, incident has offered you a bit of perspective, then?"

Chris obviously didn't approve of his new plan to win Rochelle instead of get back at her. He'd been a good friend when Rochelle had broken his heart all those years ago. He'd always made sure to get him out of the house, made sure he was eating, made sure he had his pick of women even if his heart wasn't in it. But if he didn't approve of wooing Rochelle…Well, then, it was none of Chris's business. "It certainly altered the way I feel about safety cups. And inviting women to attack me."

Chris snorted. "You could end this tonight, you know. Then enjoy a smooth sail and getting laid for the rest of the show."

"Richie would fire you on the spot if he heard you say that. What kind of show host wants a smooth sail?"

Chris shrugged. "Just looking out for you, man."

"I don't need a babysitter."

Chris made a show of eyeing his crotch and lifting a brow. "You need a freaking bodyguard."

"You volunteering?"'

Chris shrugged. "Bro's before ho's right?"

The punch was reflexive and powerful, catching Chris in the nose with a hook he never could have anticipated. His friend stumbled back a few steps, until his calf hit the edge of the fountain. He teetered, and then sprawled into the water with a pathetic little cry of surprise. A few of the crew dashed to help him. Behind Grant, the women reacted in a collective gasp. Two of them—Sakiya and Cassandra hurried to his side.

"My God, Grant, are you okay?" Sakiya said.

Cassandra ran her hand along his forearm, pushing her breasts in his face. "What happened?"

Grant smiled at them, then looked at Chris, who was being helped to his feet, coughing and sputtering, his suit dripping wet and his nose solidly broken, tiny rivulets of blood leaking their way down past his lips and chin. "Just giving our gracious host a little perspective."

He was in no mood for the Friendship Ceremony tonight as it was, and his balls still ached with a vengeance that could only be soothed by time and a regularly-applied cold compress. But Chris had overstepped his bounds, calling Rochelle a ho. It had to be done. His friend would come to realize that, and this would blow over. But for now, he just wanted this night, this entire day, to join the other bad memories he'd have of his experience on *Luring Love*. Sighing through clenched teeth, Grant motioned to the half of the camera crew still grounded in place by apparent shock. "Do we need our host to continue, or are we ready to get this ceremony over with?"

A small, fragile-looking man wearing a Nascar hat stepped out from behind one of the cameras, his expression grave. He removed his hat with reverence, as if someone had died. "Sir, I was already filming it."

R ichie leaned forward and steepled his fingers together, his glare shifting from Grant to Chris, then back at Grant. Chris stared at the ceiling, either to keep fresh blood from seeping through the cotton balls stuffed into his nostrils or because he'd already grown tired of the principal's office feel of this conversation.

Grant couldn't agree more.

"I've reviewed the film. Up until this point, I thought you two got along swimmingly. Chris, you referred Grant to the show!"

Grant focused on the rows and rows of bookshelves behind Richie's grand desk chair, trying to remember the last time he heard someone actually use the word "swimmingly".

"Some of the crew would have even called you friends," Richie continued.

Out of the corner of his eye, he saw Chris shift in his chair then sniff, never looking up at Richie.

"Neither of you has anything to say? No explanation for the playground fight on studio time?" Richie said. When he was still met with silence, he leaned back in his chair. "Christopher, you're sure you don't want an apology from Grant? By all means, we can prove that his attack was not provoked. It's all caught on tape, so to speak."

Grant raised a brow but said nothing. He hadn't noticed any sound guy hovering close to them at the time of the incident; he seriously doubted Richie could prove anything at this point. If Richie had known the words that were actually exchanged, Chris would have been in trouble for different reasons, such as suggesting Grant vote Rochelle off the show. And they certainly wouldn't have been stuck in Richie's office right now getting prodded with questions. *Probably just trying to make sure the studio itself won't be sued.*

"Nope," Chris said, popping the 'p'. But his stuffy nose made the word sound like "Dope."

Richie turned to Grant, chastising him with a scowl. "Grant, would *you* like to explain *your* behavior?"

Grant tapped his fingers on the armrest of his chair, stubbornly pursing his lips. The more questions Richie asked, the more certain he was that the producer didn't have a clue at all what had transpired on the veranda. But Grant and Chris had always had a code: Snitches get stitches. This was no different.

"Fine," Richie said, finally throwing his hands in the air. "Don't tell me what happened. But let me tell *you* something. Both of you. If it happens again, you're both off the show. All bets are off. No pay, no prize money, no bride, no happily ever after. Understood?"

Grant nodded and assumed Chris did, too, because Richie waved at them in dismissal, an overreaching, condescending gesture that showed more of his annoyance than he probably intended. "Now get out of my office."

Grant allowed Chris to lead, mostly because walking was still painful for him and his legs were stiff from keeping his manly parts arranged comfortably in the chair. As he was leaving, Richie called after him. "Grant, stay and shut the door, please?"

Chris had already made it into the hallway. He looked at Grant. "What do you think he wants now?" he whispered. But what he was really asking was if Grant was going to tell on him after all. The unspoken question lingered in the air between them, and Grant didn't mind letting Chris torture himself with the answer.

Grant shrugged. "I'll let you know. Good night."

Chris's face fell. "I'm sorry, man. I know Rochelle's not a ho."

Grant cocked a grin. "I'm sorry, too. I knew that would break your nose."

"Bastard."

Grant shut the door and turned to Richie, who by now had seated himself on the edge of his desk, a hideous smile curving at his lips. "Did it have to do with Rochelle?"

Grant shoved his hands in his pockets. *What* didn't *have to do with Rochelle?* "What, are you going to call our parents?"

Undeterred, Richie's smile widened. "Who were you going to vote off tonight?"

"Wouldn't you rather wait and be surprised?" The ceremony was put off until tomorrow. Until all injuries were at an acceptable level of swelling.

"Just tell me it's not Rochelle. She's your other half, you know. Opposites attract—"

"Spare me the pep talk. It's not Rochelle."

Richie was still cackling when Grant shut the door behind him seconds later.

Chapter Thirteen

When Grant handed Amber the bouquet of sweet peas at the Friendship Ceremony, Rochelle had to quash the urge to fling herself at him and finish the job she'd started in the gym. Her knee twitched to connect with his groin again. Over and over.

"I appreciate that you know how to defend yourself," he was telling Amber, the gorgeous fitness instructor. "But when the substitute tried to assist you in learning a new move, you completely brushed him off. To me, that says you may not be open to trying new things."

What absolute BS, Rochelle thought, shifting impatiently from one foot to the other. She'd even worn an evening gown again so she could be voted off tonight in style. But nooooo. Of course not. *Why would he vote me off? I only bludgeoned any hope he had of ever reproducing!*

She glared at him, willing him to look in her direction. But he apparently knew better. He knew not to make that mistake. Especially while the cameras were rolling. There wouldn't be an intervention for him if he provoked her tonight. Not now that Amber held the bouquet Rochelle had been so sure she'd receive. The bouquet she so desperately wanted.

"If I wasn't willing to try new things, I wouldn't have auditioned for this show," a teary-eyed Amber said. "Please. Give me another chance. I'll prove you wrong on that. I swear I will."

*Oh for the love of…*Had all these women lost their minds? *Grant?* They were groveling at the unworthy feet of Grant-Freaking-Drake? *Now I've seen it all.* He might look like something worth salivating over, but just wait until after the show and they got to know the real him.

As soon as Amber's dramatic departure from *Luring Love* ended and "Cut" was yelled, Rochelle stalked off the set and to her room, as had become her custom. Practically tearing the gown from her body, she eyed with venom the woman staring back at her in the bathroom mirror. "You're *failing*," she informed her reflection. The disappointment echoed around her but not as loudly as it reverberated inside her.

What would it take to get Grant to vote her off? Mind games didn't work. Physical assault didn't work. Murder, perhaps? Public strangulation with his own necktie? Technically, that would still win her the money for Helping Hands…

"You're still here," Maya said from behind her. "I wouldn't call that failing."

Rochelle wrenched around to face her, giving her a frantic smile while she stalled for something non-incriminating to say. "I'm not exactly winning, either," she finally countered.

"I'm not as...*sociable* as the other girls, and I think that's hurting my chances. I mean, sure, I didn't get voted off to-night, but I have a feeling it's coming. I mean, I kneed him in the rocks for God's sake." She could hardly suppress her smile at the thought. Still, doubt pirouetted in her mind. She was definitely running out of things to sabotage.

Maya crossed her arms. "*Sociable.*"

"Right. You know. Talkative."

"You were sociable enough when you opened a kissing booth, don't you think? And when you volunteered to go first for our self-defense class and for skydiving. I'd say you were plenty *sociable* then."

An unfamiliar disdain rang in Maya's voice and a mea-sure of disgust spread across her face. Was Maya jealous? Or worse, had she figured out what was going on? Out of all the other women, Maya was by far the most observant. The most self-aware, yet the most selfless. Had she been playing the game all along? Was she playing it now?

"I know what you're doing," Maya continued.

Oh God, Maya knows? I'm screwed! Rochelle imagined Richie tearing up a check in front of her face. Not getting voted off the show tonight was bad enough. *But not getting paid for all my hard work? Unacceptable.*

"Um. You do?" If Richie had to bribe Maya to stay on the show now that their cover was blown, then so be it, even if some of it had to come out of her own prize money. Just as long as she could retain most of it.

Rochelle wondered if someone as good and noble as Maya actually had a price, a bribing threshold. Or maybe, just maybe, she'd accept part of the prize money if she knew where the funds were going. A woman like Maya would probably even forfeit her own prize money for a cause as worthwhile as Helping Hands.

"I've heard of people like you," Maya spat, bringing Rochelle's concentration front and center. "People who audition for these shows just for the attention. The exposure. Let me guess, you're trying to be an actress. Or is it a model? Whatever it is, if you had any shred of decency left, you'd bow out and let those of us who actually care about this competition, about the *man* in the competition, have their shot."

So this is what everyone thinks about me. And only Maya was brave enough to step forward and officially say it, probably because Maya was the only one too honorable to talk about her behind her back. All the rest of them would just sneer and whisper, but Maya would say her peace and have done with it.

A cocktail of relief and revulsion washed over Rochelle. Her secret was still safe, but everyone on the show thought she was a camera hog and apparently a low-life. *Gross.* But she decided it would be stupid to care what the others thought. They would never see each other again after this show. These were all strangers, and none of them were worth what she'd be losing if she truly got exposed. If she gave away what was really going on, Richie wouldn't pay her a dime and all of this would have been for nothing.

Which left Rochelle with one unsavory option. "An actress," she choked out. The words tasted like a mouthful of vinegar. She raised her chin, even though the urge to hang her head in shame was almost overwhelming. Her pride would go down easier if she had time to chew it first. But she never saw this coming. "So everyone knows?" She could hear a crack in her voice and resented it. This was all pretend, every bit of it. She should have known better than to let this dumb competition get inside her head.

Maya huffed. "How can they not? You've been a drama queen from day one. The stunts you've pulled…" She shook her head. "It's very obvious, Rochelle."

"Well, then I *am* accomplishing my goal after all," she said, suddenly aware of a cameraman and sound assistant standing behind Maya, filming everything. Privacy was just a pipe dream in this place. Rochelle took the time to appear disappointed, sighing heavily. She allowed her lips to form what she hoped looked like a pout instead of duckface.

"I thought I was failing at getting noticed. Hopefully, Grant doesn't realize what I'm doing. Then he'd surely vote me off." It stung a little, that Maya obviously held her in such low esteem. And it was nauseating to be playing the part of a shallow attention whore, especially now that she knew America would see it. Richie would make sure, of that she was certain. *But I've already done things I'm not exactly proud of on this show. Why stop now? Keep playing the game and get what you came here for.*

"Maybe I should tell him," Maya said. "Someone should." But she looked doubtful. She had probably never snitched on anyone in her whole life.

Rochelle wasn't sure how to play this. If Maya did rat her out, would Grant vote her off the show? She couldn't count on that, since his motives for keeping her there were still unclear. *Would he believe I'm pursuing an acting career?* Probably not. But he *would* believe she was up to something. Still, at least the message would get through to him that she wasn't here for *him.*

But if Grant *did* vote her off after being informed of her acting endeavors, what should she make of that? *Why would he have kept me on the show this long?* Did Grant actually think they had another chance together? That they could somehow reconnect through a freaking reality show? That she would actually forgive him?

Calm down, she told herself. *Grant's feelings for you ended a long time ago, if they ever even existed in the first place. Play the game, get your money, and get out.* Not even Richie could fault her for this new turn of events. She did what she had to and got him his ratings in the process. He owed it to her to uphold their agreement if she got voted off for this. And getting voted off was still the goal, no matter how repulsive she had to be.

"Do what you think is best," Rochelle said finally, examining her nails in an attempt at appearing disinterested. "I've got to get ready for my one-on-one date with Grant tonight."

"Oh, and what will you be wearing for the occasion? A clown suit? A cheerleading outfit?"

Ouch. Under the assumed circumstances, Maya had every right to dig her claws in. But it wasn't something Rochelle expected. Truth be told, she had considered Maya a friend. Not so much anymore.

"You're risking his feelings, and you're leading him on," Maya said, angrier than ever. "But I don't suppose you've ever been hurt before. I don't suppose you know how it feels to be on the wrong side of a one-sided relationship."

Rochelle felt the blood leaving her face, pooling in her feet and hands. She could have taught classes on how it felt to be on the wrong side of a one-sided relationship. And her

mentor had been none other than Grant Drake, the object
of Maya's irrational affection. Was this really happening? "I
have to get ready for my date now," she said finally, pushing
past Maya. More of the camera crew and some of the contestants had collected in the hallway to watch. Apparently
they had expected—no, they'd *hoped* for—a catfight. She
longed to tell them where they could shove their hopes and
expectations but decided that she'd made enough enemies
for the evening, especially if Maya had finally turned against
her and become their spokesperson.

So instead, she made her way to the closet to prepare
for her date.

Chapter Fourteen

Grant waited in the chef-level kitchen of the mansion. Rochelle was, naturally, running late for their one-on-one date. But he didn't care. He finally had some time with her alone. And he had a lot to say. Richie would likely have a conniption. Chris would probably cut more than he filmed. Chris had likely gotten used to this routine.

Grant leaned against the counter and watched the camera crew make some last-minute adjustments to their equipment. The ingredients spread before him on the countertop made him salivate, even though he knew they could never be combined in a palatable way if Rochelle was the one responsible for weaving this into something edible. A pile of sweet potatoes, a bowl of raw chicken, small glass bowls of carefully measured spices and a carton of sour cream all awaited their certain demise. It could have been the recipe for something wonderful—if Rochelle didn't step foot in the kitchen.

That's not fair. Sure, she didn't know how to butter toast when we were together but now she could be a top-notch cook. Rochelle had changed since college after all. She used to be sweet and easygoing, up for anything. But she'd also been ambitious and no-nonsense when it came to things that mattered to her. The aggressive tendencies had gained dominance over sweet and easygoing, but he was sure that old charming Chelle was still under there somewhere. And he had to bring her back.

Still, he hoped the new Rochelle Ransom—the one he prayed was a spatula-wielding ninja in the kitchen—showed up to turn this mess into something delicious because he was starving. After a full stomach, maybe he could go about bringing out the old charming Chelle he loved.

But his hope for a satisfying meal only stretched so far. She had been a terrible cook in college. Even his mother hadn't been able to teach her how to bake, and that was saying something. Not only had her cookies turned out salty for some reason, they had also looked a lot like biscuits. The memory brought a smile to his face. She'd been so upset. He'd had to choke three of them down before she could be consoled. Not that he minded consoling her of course, which usually involved holding and kissing her and distracting her from breathing in general.

It was then that he saw it. And his smile faded.

There, next to the bowl labeled "White Pepper." He squinted; he had to be certain. *It can't be.*

But it was. The label screamed at him, mocking him from across the kitchen. *Chopped Walnuts.*

Rochelle was very aware of his allergy to walnuts. She knew he broke out into bulbous hives which eventually overtook his body, causing him to itch more than if he'd been attacked by a swarm of mosquitos. That was *if* he didn't take his daily allergy medicine—which he did now.

It was much easier to take the medication on a regular basis than risk having an attack at some random restaurant where the server didn't know what was in the food and possibly didn't care. Back when he and Rochelle had been together, they rarely had the money to eat out, so they cooked in their dorm rooms and ordered pizza. Avoiding walnuts had been easy, something they did as second nature. The first time they did go out to a fancy dinner, Grant's allergy flared up in full force because of something in the sauce prepared with his salmon and Rochelle had insisted he go straight to the emergency room, even though his symptoms had subsided after he'd used his EpiPen. And now she was going to serve his allergy to him on a silver platter?

The vindictive little brat. Nothing had changed, had it? Rochelle hadn't learned to cook. Why would she? She lived the life of a busy, single attorney. Who was there to cook for? That meant only one thing. *She intends to prepare me a horrendous meal to begin with, force me to eat it, then laugh as I humiliate myself when I break out into sudden leprosy. Either that,* or *she'll make me refuse and humiliate her on national television.*

He clenched his teeth. *Not this time, Rochelle Ransom.*

Chapter Fifteen

Grant is in an irritatingly good mood tonight, Rochelle thought to herself as she set to mashing up the baked sweet potatoes. He sat on one of the barstools across from her, swirling a glass of wine in one hand, and gesturing with another while he told his story about how he stopped traffic to save a turtle from crossing the interstate. The only thing he omitted from the tale was that she had been there with him at the time—and *she* was the one who'd insisted they save the poor thing.

It was yet another reason she was glad she had the option to cook him a meal. They both knew she couldn't cook. That he was even sitting here calmly suggested he may not remember. *Or maybe he thinks I've learned to cook after all this time. Poor him.* She nearly giggled aloud. The best part was, the studio provided the recipe—so when all this reached its gruesome conclusion, and Grant took his first bite of nastiness, she could blame it on the studio and not her lack of cooking know-how. Delighted, she added the rest of the ingredients to the pot per the recipe, folding the potatoes over and over until it became one solid mixture. It was the ugliest batch of mashed sweet potatoes she'd ever seen. Even the texture was questionable, she thought happily.

She became aware of the lack of noise coming from Grant's general direction. When she looked up, he was already grinning at her. "What?" she said, feeling instant uneasiness when his expression changed to one she was very familiar with. One with actual emotion in it.

"Rochelle… Since we're enjoying some time alone with each other, I'd hoped it would afford us the chance to get to know each other better."

She set the masher in the sink and pretended to check the jerk chicken in the oven. She had no idea what it was supposed to look like at this point, but she'd do anything right now to avoid looking directly at him. "Okay. What did you have in mind?"

"Well, if I can be frank with you, it seems like you have a wall built up around you. I notice that you don't interact much with the other girls — or with me, for that matter."

"Really? I've felt like we've bonded these past few weeks."

His smile faltered while his eyes darted to the camera and back. "We've been in some intimate situations, that's for sure. But nothing that afforded us any time to talk. So, I thought we could play Twenty Questions."

Omigod, we have to talk? Like, really talk? So far this evening the conversation had been minimal, since she'd made the excuse that she couldn't concentrate on cooking and talk at the same time. Grant had been very obliging, probably because he'd planned to pull this on her when she was done preparing dinner.

Rochelle looked to Chris, who stood next to one of the side cameras. *Did you put him up to this?* she accused with her eyes. In response he gave her an innocent shrug. Lovely. She'd be getting no assistance from the show's host tonight. Not that she'd exactly been nice to him. Or cooperative. Or civilized…

So then, she was on her own. She could handle this. How bad could it get, anyway? She cleared her throat and looked back at Grant. He allowed her time to compose a neutral expression, though she doubted the camera missed how startled she was at the prospect of small talk.

"Sounds fun," she gritted out.

"Great," he said charismatically. "So, question number one. Have you ever made a mistake that changed your life?"

She folded her hands on the counter in front of her and stared at them for long enough to make the moment awkward. Chris would appreciate the tension, she knew. "Wow. You go straight for the deep end of the pool, don't you?"

He gave a small laugh, as if she'd told a joke. "I told you I was going to be frank."

Her head snapped up, and she met his gaze. Heat crept up her neck and into her face. The camera wouldn't be missing that either. "Yes, you did," she said finally. He had no idea how blunt she could be. Grant had never had the pleasure of watching her corner a witness in the courtroom. He deserved a little taste of that, she decided. "I once dated this jackass who completely broke my heart."

At this Grant flinched. *You started this*, she said with her eyes.

He nodded as if in acknowledgement, as if taking responsibility. "Okay. That's interesting, and I'd certainly like to know more about it, but it's your turn. Do you have a question for me?"

It sickened her to realize that she'd been hoping for more of a reaction from him. And she'd been hoping the reaction involved torment and pain and regret. But noooo. He'd started a game he wasn't really interested in playing. Why? For Richie's ratings? Whatever the case, she didn't want to play, either. "What's your favorite color?" she asked, attempting to appear bored.

Slowly he shook his head. "No. Let's move past those kinds of questions and really get to the heart of each other. Ask me something else."

The oven beeped then, and she offered him a half-hearted smile. "Excuse me," she said, turning away from him. "The chicken is ready." *Get to the heart of each other?* That didn't work out so well last time. A sense of dread seeped throughout her. Would he really bring up their personal past? Would he really make her face it in front of the crew, in front of Chris, or worse, in front of America? Surely Chris would cut it or at the very least edit the conversation into an unrecognizable version of itself.

The next few minutes were filled with silence. With shaking hands, Rochelle served them both dinner. Grant allowed her time enough to take her apron off, sit at the table with him, and sip her wine. But he wouldn't be put off any longer. Grant had never been good at being put off. "Rochelle? Your question?"

She sighed and downed the rest of the wine, setting the empty glass firmly on the table. They were really going to have this conversation, in code, on national television. Fine. But it wasn't going to be a cakewalk for him. She would make sure of that. "My question is the same. Have you ever made a mistake that changed your—"

"Yes," he said. "I broke up with the woman I loved. The woman I was going to marry. Or so I'd thought."

Marry? Surely he wasn't talking about her. He had to be some sort of serial dater, breaking hearts along whatever path life had taken him these past years. Hell, within hours of their breakup, he'd already had his hands on another woman.

Rochelle swallowed. Hard. "And why would you do that? Break up with her, I mean."

This time Grant was the one who looked away. He shuffled the potatoes around the plate with his fork. He had yet to take a bite. "She had bigger and better things to move on to."

He's not talking about me. He couldn't have been, because she never would have left him for someone else. To her, Grant had been all there was. There had been no one else. Not for her. Not then, and not since.

Grant scooped up the potatoes and shoveled them into his mouth, slamming his fork on the plate. "She's the whole reason I'm even on this show," he said with a full mouth. "No woman has ever lived up to her. My love life has been screwed up ever since she left."

She stood abruptly, sending her chair flying backward. "Left? *You* left *her* the second you broke up with her!" This was getting too personal to talk in code anymore. *Surely America sees what's really happening here. Surely they know there's something between us.* "Then you had your hands and mouth all over another woman!" Oh God, had she said that out loud?

She'd promised herself she'd never think of it again, never bring those images back into her mind. The truth was, he'd kissed another girl that same night. She'd never forget watching him through the pub window. She'd come back to make amends, to tell him that she simply wasn't going to accept his breakup. Oh, how stupid she had felt when she saw Tiffany Wallace sit on his lap and kiss him senseless. How her heart and hopes and dreams had ruptured like an egg dropped on the floor.

Tiffany. Freaking. Wallace. The girl was easier than the alphabet.

"What are you talking about? I would never have left her, and never for another woman." He ran a hand through his hair. "I mean, there were women after her, but none that I cared about. No, *she* left *me* for something better."

"Oh yes, I keep forgetting you're playing the 'she-was-moving-on' card." Whatever that meant. Moving on to what?

"It's true," he said, pounding a fist on the table.

Chris cleared his throat loud enough to startle a corpse.

"You don't know what happened, of course," Grant reminded her softly. "You weren't there, remember?"

Calm down, idiot. You're about to lose everything. "Of course I wasn't there," she snapped. "I can only imagine. But it's no stretch to see you after a breakup, going to a local bar and hanging all over the town whore." Whose name was Tiffany Wallace!

Grant squared his shoulders. "The town who—" His face fell. *Yes, that's right, Grant Drake. I saw you!* Now he's remembering the events as they really happened, she can tell.

"That? You might not believe it, Rochelle, but women do flirt with me on occasion. And I'm not going to treat them disrespectfully," Grant said.

Disrespectfully? He should have pushed her to the floor and sent her on her way! But, she admitted, that wasn't Grant's style. And she hadn't stuck around to see how he'd handled it. She'd just assumed the kiss was a welcome assault.

He ran a hand through his hair. "I would have done anything to save the relationship. But by that point, it was over and I knew it."

"Save the relationship? When you were so bent on ending it? I mean, that's the impression I get, anyway." America was going to think she was a psychic if she kept throwing out tidbits of information like that. So, she was forced to rein in her temper yet again. She retrieved her chair and pulled it back to the table, sitting down carefully. Sometimes composure could be a slippery slope. "So, I think it's your turn to ask a question."

He speared the chicken with his fork. He seemed taken aback and confused. *What, he didn't even remember what had happened that night? Give me a break.* Still, though, something was bothering him, she could tell. Other than the one bite, he hadn't touched his food. Obviously he recalled how well she couldn't cook. "Tell me about your family," he said.

Rochelle straightened in her chair, trying not to visibly bristle. "My father is in jail, actually." But he already knew that. Grant was the one who put him there. He made the phone call she had always been too scared to place. The Sheriff's department had come. Her mother had been taken away by ambulance. Grant had made the call. He'd been strong enough for the both of them.

"And your mother?"

"She died two years ago. Complications of pneumonia." Though in spirit, her mother had died long before that. Rochelle had moved her into her apartment in the city to look after her. Her mother's health had kept fading and fading, until she was a mere wisp of the person she used to be before her husband decided to use her as a punching bag.

Tears welled in Rochelle's eyes. Should she have called Grant when her mother died? What would she have said? And what if he'd acted callously again?

Grant wiped a hand down his face, pausing to pinch the bridge of his nose. "God, Rochelle, I'm so sorry. I didn't know."

"Of course you didn't," she said, looking at the napkin in her lap. "How could you?" A fat tear spilled over but she wiped it away quickly. Grant had liked her mom, and she'd liked him. Grant had saved her mom's life.

Damn him for acting like an emotional nitwit and damn him for turning her into one.

"Was it…did she…?" he said, clearly flustered by the limitations governing their exchange.

"I'd rather talk about something else, if you don't mind."

He sighed, nodding. A few moments passed that felt like centuries. Absently, he took another bite of his potatoes. "I believe it's your turn to ask me a question."

Find a question, find a question, find a question. Any question but the one you're thinking of right now. But it came out anyway. "You said you wanted to marry the woman you broke up with." *Don't ask questions you shouldn't care about anymore.*

"Yes, I did. I already had a ring."

She filed that away for later, only allowing the shock to hit the surface. She couldn't deal with what that meant, not in front of the cameras and Chris Schnartz-Legend and especially not in front of Grant. Truth be told, she wasn't sure if she could deal with it at all. A ring. He'd had a ring to give her. That is, if she was the one he was talking about. "If… if you could find this woman again, if you could look her in the eyes right now, what would you say to her?" She took a bite of her potatoes, just in case her mouth wanted to ask any other stupid questions. And then she tasted the familiar crunch of walnut.

She'd grown sensitive to it, always acting as Grant's taste tester back when they had dated since Grant was severely allergic to walnuts. He broke out in horrifying welts all over his body, and sometimes his throat even closed up, depending on how much he'd eaten. And she had dumped an entire bowl full in those freaking sweet potatoes. "Omigod Grant," she said, dropping her fork. "This has walnuts in it!"

Grant didn't seem the least bit fazed. He questioned her with a look. "You knew it had walnuts in it. You put them in yourself."

"I was following the recipe, you idiot! How much did you eat?" Because timing from when he took his first bite until now…he'd be showing signs very soon.

He cast a worried glance at the still-rolling cameras. "And it was delicious, really," he said pointedly.

Wait, what? Why was he stalling? He knew what was going to happen. Did he really want that to go down on television? This was life or death, and he was still trying to play the part of strangers talking over dinner! *And why do I care?* "Grant, how much did you eat?"

"You know, I knew someone once who had an allergy to peanuts," he said casually sipping his wine. "He takes medicine for it now, though. Doesn't bother him at all." His look couldn't be more meaningful.

Medicine. Doesn't bother him at all. "Oh. Right." She didn't realize until now that she was clutching at her throat. She released herself and tried her best to appear relaxed in the chair—a feat as difficult as nailing pudding to the wall. "I, uh, thought I put too much in it for a second there. You didn't think it tasted strong?" Totally lame and totally un-believable, but Chris hadn't yelled cut yet. In fact, he stood there looking rather pleased. He knew what happened when Grant ate walnuts, too. Had he known the recipe called for them?

In transparent relief, Grant said, "Not at all. It was delicious. The chicken is great, too."

The potatoes tasted like dirt and butter whipped together into a paste, and the chicken was drier than a mouthful of sand sprinkled with teriyaki sauce. He was lying, and they both knew it. What bothered her the most, though, was the fact that he apparently *knew* she'd put walnuts in it, and he ate the potatoes anyway. He must have thought she'd done it on purpose. And why wouldn't he think that? For God's sake, she'd done everything else in her power to humiliate him, but her intentions were never to kill the idiot.

Is this what he thought of her now? And why, why, why did it bother her?

For a few moments, they just stared at each other. What was the next move? Whose turn was it to play the part?

Should she say something? But she was too rattled to open her mouth. The least Grant could do was change the subject so they could get this dinner rolling again and ultimately over with. Even Chris began to fidget from his position just outside the view of the camera. The parts he could actually keep of this segment were rife with awkward silences and uncomfortable glances. He cleared his throat several times, but she was too mortified with herself to act. Grant seemed perfectly at ease, if not a little perplexed.

That's when the ridiculousness of the situation settled in. All of it, since the beginning of the show. Everything she'd been doing. His efforts to deflect her wrath. Their mutual, if somewhat misplaced, determination to come out on top. They had been so competitive that a simple mistake had been misinterpreted as attempted murder.

And all at once Rochelle burst out laughing. It didn't take long for Grant to join in, his deep bellows resounding throughout the kitchen. They laughed so hard and for so long that the camera crew began to get antsy. She was quite certain Chris was already editing this part in his head. Why he didn't just cut the entire scene was beyond her.

"You thought I did it on purpose!" Rochelle said, breathless.

"Well you can see why, can't you," Grant said, wiping a tear from the corner of his eye.

Now she was gulping for air. So he *had* noticed her efforts to sabotage him. And he'd planned accordingly this evening...for premeditated murder? "*Why* would you eat it?"

"I was covered! At least, I was hoping..."

They both let loose another explosion of laughter.

Rochelle gripped the table, as if doing so would help her breathe in steadier streams of air. Grant's face flushed, either with the force of his laughter or the force of his embarrassment.

"Remember that one time at the pub when your throat closed up and we were trying to decide which of us was most qualified to perform a trachea?" And the qualifications had been directly related to how much they had drunk in relation to their body weight.

Grant nods. "And Colby came at me with the sharpened straw and I knocked him unconscious!"

"We had to take you both to the hospital," Rochelle recalled with glee. "And your mom had to come get us in the van!"

"I think that's a wrap," Chris said irritably from the crew line. Exasperation radiated from him as he walked to the table. He gave Rochelle the once over, then rested his accusatory gaze on Grant who was still guffawing. When it became apparent Chris had something he felt was particularly important to say, Grant calmed down, though a broad smile stayed plastered on his face.

"You two are so weird," Chris informed him.

Weird. It was what he'd always called them when they were dating—and it was usually when they were acting particularly in love.

In love.

And with that, reality washed over her. Of course he thought they were weird. They'd been at each other's throats for weeks, and now they sat laughing together over a potentially deadly mishap. Plus, he knew their past. Why they were at odds. And now he was probably confused as to why they weren't.

Except, they still were. She couldn't let Grant's admission mean anything to her. She couldn't let herself feel anything for this man again. Could she?

Yes, they were weird indeed. Weird and pathetic. She was just sitting here laughing with Grant as if they didn't have a dark past. For a few precious moments, it had been like old times. Except, it could never be like old times again. Not really. And they'd both do well to remember that.

Standing, she placed the napkin on the plate and scooted her chair out. "Thanks, Chris. If that's all you need for the shoot, then please excuse me."

"Chelle—" Grant said, standing, too. There was pleading in his eyes, and it made her remember that he had bought a ring and was going to ask her to marry him...until he'd suddenly broken up with her for no apparent reason? To move on to better things? What was that supposed to mean? It made her remember everything she had lost and the pain she had gone through to heal. And she wasn't ready to do that again.

"Don't call me Chelle." She turned on her heel and walked away.

Chapter Sixteen

Progress had been made, Grant was sure of it. Otherwise, Rochelle wouldn't have been trying so much harder to get voted off the show. He snuck a glance at her from across the dinner table, careful not to let Ellie, the other contestant on their two-on-one date, see him.

Grant cringed. It looked like someone had given a monkey a paintbrush and instructed it to use Rochelle's face as a canvas. That, or a birthday cake up had upchucked on her.

And her dress was decidedly hideous. All geometric shapes and colors and apparently the material was cut from a burlap sack and dyed to within an inch of its life. Of course, he should have been thankful that she was wearing a dress at all, instead of that traitorous, rancid sweatshirt she was so fond of.

She could act like a court jester all she wanted. She'd opened up to him during dinner the other night, if only for a moment. And as far as he could glean from their conversation, his biggest obstacle with her was Tiffany Wallace. Yes, he'd gone out drinking with friends after the breakup. Yes, he'd had too much to drink, and yes, Tiffany Wallace had kissed him. Obviously this is the part Rochelle saw when she came back for him. If only she'd seen him pry Tiffany off of himself and call her a cab. If only she'd seen that he didn't kiss Tiffany back.

Oh sure, he'd wanted to kiss Tiffany. He'd wanted her to make his pain go away. He'd wanted to take comfort in her arms and in her body, wanted to use her just as she intended to use him. But he couldn't. Not with the image of Rochelle walking away from him at the restaurant burning so brightly in his mind.

Thankfully, Ellie interrupted his darkening mood with an easy question. "So, Grant, have you dined here before? I was hoping for help with the menu."

Grant relaxed instantly. He'd already played this game several times this week with other contestants. This was the last two-on-one date before the next Friendship Ceremony. It had been awkward to say the least. The show thought it would be entertaining to pair type-A personalities with type-B personalities; the results had been...interesting. Lobster bisque ended up in a contestant's lap, another contestant somehow inadvertently admitted to having a taste for live worms, and yet another one questioned Grant's personal choices in life because he'd ordered a rib-eye.

This particular date should have been effortless for him. After all, Rochelle would feel obligated to sit there like a corpse and not engage in conversation, the way she always did. And when Ellie saw that Rochelle had stepped down, she'd feel more at ease and hopefully somewhat pleasant. After all, she was a kindergarten teacher. Weren't kindergarten teachers *supposed* to be pleasant? *Plus, if she misbehaves on the show, her job could be in jeopardy or something like that, right?*

He hoped that was the case. "Sorry to say I haven't. I'm not from around here, and they've been taking us to different restaurants this week."

"Oh well," she said prettily. "I guess I'll have to be adventurous." She gave him what felt like a practiced smile. Ellie was one of the more down-to-earth contestants. In fact, she and Maya seemed to be the only sane ones on board. Everyone else felt so...predatory. Except of course, for Rochelle who was about as predatory as the limp napkin splayed across his lap.

"Tell me, Ellie," Grant said for conversation's sake. "Do you enjoy eating out or do you like quiet dinners at home?"

Something in her eyes changed. Like an instant detachment. "Both, I suppose."

Possibly the most boring answer she could have given. Grant tried again. "What has been your favorite date so far on the show?"

And just like that, she sparked to life again. "I'd have to say the giant garden maze. It reminded me of my class back home. Creating mazes and such."

"Do you enjoy teaching kindergarten?"

"I love it. I love children. Do...do you enjoy children?"

Ellie was more forward than he'd expected. Good for her. "I do. I hope to have some one day. With the right woman, of course." This seemed like an echo from their Cozy Couch session. But it wasn't Ellie he was hoping to make an impression on. Still, he didn't dare let his gaze stray to Chelle. Out of the corner of his eye, though, he saw her head snap up. So, the subject of children still interested her.

It didn't surprise him. There had been a time when the two of them had a pregnancy scare. Rochelle had been a few days late and before she took the test, they both allowed themselves to ponder over "what if" together. Both of them agreed they'd keep the baby. That they'd make it work. Grant never told her how disappointed he was when the test had come back negative. It was something he'd wanted with her, something he hadn't realize he'd wanted so badly until it was a real possibility. But he'd told himself to be patient. That they had the rest of their lives. And suddenly they didn't.

"Rochelle? What about you? Do you want children one day?" he asked, the nostalgia making his voice softer than he'd intended.

She stiffened. On the table, her fist clenched. "With the right man, of course."

He pursed his lips. He knew she was thinking back to the same moment in time he was. To a time when having a child with him was exciting and new. He wondered what feelings the memory conjured up for her. "We keep saying the 'right' man or the 'right' woman. What in your opinion, ladies, would the 'right' man be like?"

"Committed," Rochelle snapped.

Ellie nodded emphatically. "Yes, committed of course. But he would have to be kind. And of course, he'd have to love children, and he couldn't be overly materialistic..." While Ellie rambled on, Grant noticed that Rochelle's eyes were glossing over with un-spilled tears. He cast her a worried look. She shook her head, then sipped her wine, visibly tuning out of the conversation.

How can I get through to her that I am *committed?* That hurting her was the last thing he ever wanted to do? That he'd thought he was doing the best thing for her? That all he'd been trying to do was make the decision to go to law school easy for her? She hadn't seemed to pick up on his meaning during their one-on-one date the other night. How else could he get through to her without actually saying it on camera? They needed a direct conversation, to get everything out in the open, and they needed it soon. Maybe Chris would help him arrange it without Richie knowing…

It took a minute for him to realize that Ellie was now crying. Jesus, and he thought tonight was going to be the easiest. He was more than surprised to find that Rochelle had reached across the table and took Ellie's hand in hers, rubbing it gently with her thumb.

"You got pretty specific with your requirements for the right man," Rochelle was saying softly. "Have you been married before, Ellie?"

Ellie sniffled. "Am I that obvious?"

"I'm afraid so, sweetie," Rochelle said. "But if you don't want to talk about it, we don't have to."

Grant blinked. Was this the same mass-destruction Rochelle who had been on the show these past weeks? Was she actually *nurturing* Ellie?

Ellie turned to Grant. "I'm so sorry, Grant. I should have told you sooner than this. I owe you that much. I thought…I thought the show would be good for me."

"Ellie," Grant said, putting his arm around her. He hated to see a woman cry and would have done anything to make it stop. "Rochelle is right. If you don't want to do this right now, we don't have to. Whatever it is, it's obvious that it causes you pain to talk about it. You don't owe me anything."

"I was married," Ellie blurted. "To the most 'right' man on the planet. Every Friday night he brought me home flowers. We drew straws to see if we would go out or stay in that night. He volunteered at my school." Grant wished there was a balm to put on the rawness that was her voice. He exchanged solemn glances with Rochelle. The best thing to do seemed to let Ellie talk it out. At least he and Rochelle agreed on something.

"I was going to buy him a motorcycle for our anniversary," she said, still sniffling. "Just take him to the dealership and let him pick one out. But two weeks before—a Friday— he came home without flowers for me. That's when I first knew something was wrong. He'd forgotten them, you see. Because of the news he'd gotten at the doctor's office. All it took was six months," she sobbed. "Six months and he was gone." She broke down then, without reserve.

Grant closed his eyes against the frantic urge to pull her to him and comfort her. No wonder she hadn't wanted to talk about eating out or staying in; it had been a tradition, something special she had shared with her husband.

"What happened, Ellie?" Rochelle said. To Grant's relief, Rochelle inched closer to Ellie, shackling her in a huge embrace. It was better that Rochelle do it. He didn't want to give Ellie the wrong impression, and he certainly didn't want to set Rochelle off at a time like this.

Though, by the way she was acting, Rochelle wouldn't think of acting out right now. She was all sympathetic and soothing. He hadn't seen this side of her for a very long time. His heart ached with what else he'd missed out on all these years.

"Cancer. It's been a little over a year," Ellie choked. "A year and three months. Oh God, I'm so sorry. I'm ruining our date."

"Trust me, Ellie, neither one of us thinks that, do we Grant?" Rochelle said.

"No way," Grant said. "It took a lot of courage to come on this show. I think you're so much stronger than you realize, Ellie. I think your husband would be proud."

Ellie offered a tiny, clogged-up laugh. "Proud that I've been prancing around on some dating show?"

"Proud that you're trying to go on with life. He would want that. I'm absolutely certain."

"Oh God, you're so nice, too," she said sadly. "If only I weren't still married in my head. You would be such a catch."

Grant smiled. "Don't be ridiculous, Ellie. It's me who's missing out."

Chapter Seventeen

Rochelle made her way down to the makeup studio set up in one of the many living rooms of the mansion. She was met with surprise as Tommy—at least, that was what his nametag said—one of the makeup artists, clicked his tongue. "Did you get lost in the mansion, honey? I haven't seen you down here before."

She should have expected to catch flack for finally going down there. "I'm testing out the 'appropriate' look for tonight's Friendship Ceremony."

He placed the back of his hand to her forehead. "No fever. Did you take your meds this morning?"

"What meds?" she said irritably, sitting in the chair in front of Tommy's mirror. She was in no mood for sarcasm.

"The meds that made you think that blouse goes with that skirt. Oh wait, but that's your style, isn't it?"

She examined the mirror then, sighing heavily. She kind of *had* thought the blouse went with the skirt. But Tommy seemed better informed on such things than she was. "I'll go down to Wardrobe after you're done with me."

Tommy raised an elegant brow. "Think you're getting voted off tonight? Wanting to make a glamorous exit?"

"I think I'm getting voted off at *every* Friendship Ceremony." The truth was, this was her new plan of attack. If Grant was repulsed by her ridiculous outfits and appalling makeup, he hadn't shown it outwardly. Which meant she had just been embarrassing herself instead of pissing him off.

Plus, she'd been thinking a lot about their conversation on their one-on-one date. He'd said he had planned to ask her to marry him. That he had bought the ring and everything. So there *had* been something between them. She hadn't imagined the whole thing back then. It was something special, too, even apparently to Grant.

So why did he have to throw it all away?

A deep ache settled in her chest. There was no point in asking "why" anymore. Hadn't she learned that already? The fact was, he *had* thrown it all away and so heartlessly that she couldn't forgive him. Maybe her mind could, especially after the way he delicately handled Ellie's meltdown last night. But her heart was the problem. Her heart was the true casualty.

Because, God help her, her heart still wanted vengeance.

Since Grant hadn't voted her off the show, he obviously wanted her there — a fact that had been perplexing her for all these weeks. But after their dinner, after their conversation, she began to realize why he wanted her to stay.

Grant Drake thought there was still a chance between them.

And she decided she was going to let him think that.

"Make me look gorgeous, Tommy," she said. "I have a bachelor to impress."

Two hours, three wardrobe changes, and one makeup session later, Rochelle emerged from her room in her low-cut periwinkle cocktail dress. Her breasts screamed to be covered up, but her heart told them, *Man up, we're on a mission*. Her hair splayed over her shoulders, flat-ironed into submission, then curled into a feminine creation she could never have achieved at home.

She made her way down the staircase; negotiating those stairs was more life-threatening in stilettos than it had ever been in tennis shoes, she decided. She'd timed her entrance to the veranda just right—late, and last. To file out in single line, to be one with the other contestants just wouldn't do. Not if she was going to draw the most attention.

When she reached the double French doors, she took a deep breath. They were all used to her being late, of course. But what they weren't used to was her looking like one of them. Like she actually wanted to be there. Sure, she'd donned dresses before. But she'd never been done up. She'd never been…well, stunning. The other contestants weren't used to her playing the game. She knew they'd all written her off as an eventual bouquet recipient and had turned their noses up at her. And it was going to feel good to prove them wrong.

As she stepped out onto the cobblestone, she could immediately tell her companions didn't like the new her. Gasps and sneers followed her as she made her way *in front* of them to the end of the line.

Huzzah, skanks.

She made steady eye contact with Grant—which was easy to do because he was staring at her, mouth ajar—and gave him a shy smile. Then she fixed a sexy expression on her face that she hoped didn't actually appear constipated because of the way she kept her head tilted slightly to the side.

"And we're rolling!" Chris called from the ranks of the crew. His smirk let her know he had acknowledged her change of attitude as well. *He probably thinks I'm coming around.*

Grant seemed startled, tearing his gaze from her and clearing his throat. "Um, good evening, ladies," he said with a generic smile. "You all look lovely, as usual." With this, he glanced pointedly at Rochelle, as if to give her his approval. She widened her smile, trying not to actually fall forward in the stilettos. A face-plant would have been rather inconvenient at the moment.

"It's been a long and interesting week," Grant continued. "All in all, I think the two-on-one dates went very well. It gave me the chance to get to know each one of you so much better, to really catch a glimpse of what you have on the inside."

Rochelle put effort into not rolling her eyes, but she felt her left one twitching. Silently, she prayed her false eyelashes would hold on tight.

"Sure, there were some mishaps, but you all handled it in stride this week. But that's not the reason my decision came so easily to me this time. I didn't have to think twice about it, really." Here, Grant paused for effect like an expert. She saw one of the cameramen focusing in on his face.

Rochelle followed Grant's line of sight to Ellie. *Oh no.* Surely he wouldn't vote her off after that emotional breakdown last night. Was he really that heartless? Then she remembered a certain last dinner they'd shared ten years ago. Yep, he was.

"Maya, please step forward," Grant said.

Her inhale was audible as Maya did as she was asked. She squared her shoulders, not intimidated at all at the possibility of being voted off. Rochelle still wished they could have been friends.

"Maya, I've come to really admire you. You're one of the contestants I think about the most."

What?

"I think about how down-to-earth you are," Grant continued, taking her hand. "And what a good sport you've been through some of the setbacks we've had on the show. That's why I'm not giving you the bouquet tonight. I hope to get to know you better during our one-on-one date next week."

Maya threw her arms around Grant, at which Rochelle swallowed an unwelcome sentiment. Jealousy had no room in this new game she was playing.

"I admire you, too," Maya said. Then she stepped away and all but swaggered back to the other contestants.

Did I misread him? Is he falling for Maya? What is happening here?

"Rochelle, please step forward."

Dear God, was he going to vote her off tonight, just when she'd decided she wanted to stay? Just when she'd formed the perfect plan to finally take vengeance on him?

He took her hands in his, but the action felt insignificant

to her now, non-personal. After all, he did just have another woman's hands in his, not thirty seconds before. She felt her own heartbeat in her ears, her lips. *He's going to vote me off.*

It was a bit disappointing. She'd wanted to see how far Grant would go to win her back. Apparently not very far. *But you still get the prize money. And you get to go back to your normal, quiet life.* It was just that something about "normal" and "quiet" made her existence sound so...stale.

"Rochelle, I know you've had a hard time adjusting to life on the show. At first, I thought you and I would never work together, but I was wrong. After our one-on-one date the other night, I felt a connection to you—something I haven't felt in years."

Don't let his words get to you.

Don't let his words get to you.

Don't let his words get to you.

"I've been thinking a lot about the last question you asked me on our date night that I never got to answer. You asked if I could find this woman again, if I could look her in the eyes right now, what would I say to her. I appreciate how deep the question was, but at the time, when put on the spot, I probably would have given a stupid answer. Since then, though, I've had time to think about that question. And I wanted to answer it for you tonight."

She drew in a sharp breath. An almost-overwhelming reflex overtook her, the unmistakable urge to turn and run as fast as her stilettos could take her over cobblestone. But she couldn't run. He was forcing her to hear him. *They're just words. Words that mean nothing!*

Right?

"This is what I would say to her." He squeezed her hands

in a meaningful way, one that he'd used when he'd wanted something of her. A kiss, an acknowledgement, an embrace. More times than not, it was a signal that he wanted to take her to his bed. He always followed it by running his fingers lightly along her wrist, just as he was doing now.

Run, she told herself. *Run away.* But she was trapped by the studio lights, by the throng of contestants behind them, by the thought of Richie tearing up a hefty check in front of her.

"I would say that not one day has passed that I haven't thought about her," Grant continued. "Not one day has gone by that I didn't regret what I did. Not one second has passed that I haven't loathed myself for losing everything I'd ever wanted in one night. But I would want her to know that, given the chance, I would do everything in my power to make it up to her. All I need is a chance."

Slowly, Rochelle pulled her hands from his. She was pretty sure he could tell how hard her heart was pounding. She felt tears sting the back of her eyes but wouldn't let them escape. "Why did you even volunteer for this show if you're still hung up on someone else?" Why was she asking questions that didn't matter again?

At this, Grant took pause. She couldn't tell if he was doing it for the sake of the show or if she had really stumped him. "Because she left a hole in me, and I hoped that someone else could fill it."

"Let's hope someone can," she said, nearly choking on the words. So much for taking vengeance. She should have been using this opportunity to be tempting and teasing and eager, yet she'd shied away from him again. She should have taken control of the situation, instead of cowering under the weight of her feelings. Her *feelings*.

Feelings did not belong in this game.

She backed away then, turning and walking to the line of very confused contestants. Grant had just admitted—on his own dating show, no less—that he was still in love with someone else. And that someone else could possibly be her. She wondered what the other women were thinking right now.

Screw the other women—what am I supposed to be thinking? But she knew deep down, it was anything but what she was thinking—that she might still be in love with him, too. Why else would she have been trying so hard to get away from him?

To her relief, Grant didn't look at Rochelle again. In fact, he didn't look at any of the contestants. He simply walked to the stone pedestal and picked up the bouquet of sweet peas. He sighed. "Ellie, please step forward."

Rochelle couldn't tell from her view, but she thought Ellie might have been sniffling as she walked to where Grant stood with the flowers. The inconvenience of conflicting emotions overwhelmed Rochelle. On the one hand, she was glad not to have been eliminated. On the other, did it *have* to be Ellie? Couldn't he have held out for one more episode, just so she could save face? "Ellie, my reason for eliminating you tonight is a bit hypocritical of me. Your heart is just not available. Not yet. But I'm convinced that one day it will be. And that one day, you'll find the right man again." Gently, he handed her the bouquet.

Rochelle shook her head, livid. *How can he do this? He's voting her off just when she needs a boost of reassurance.*

Grant reached into the pocket of his tux and produced

an envelope, handing it to Ellie. "I've created a foundation in your husband's name, Ellie. Its purpose is to help grieving spouses cope with their loss. I've named you the president. Inside, you'll find my contribution check. The producers of *Luring Love* have decided to match it. My condolences again for your loss. I hope you know I value your friendship."

Ellie collapsed against his chest. "Thank you, Grant. Thank you so much."

He embraced her, holding her as if she were a child. Rochelle swallowed a sob of her own. "You're very welcome."

Ellie pulled back then, wiping her face with both hands in an attempt to correct the river of mascara running down her cheeks. Rochelle didn't try to hold back her own tears, false lashes or no. Neither did the rest of the contestants. It was an emotional gesture for all in attendance. Even Chris watched grimly from his position, nodding slightly in approval.

"You're a good man, Grant," Ellie said. "A good man. Just not the right one for me. Thank you for the flowers. They're beautiful."

Chris stepped onto the veranda and placed his hand on Ellie's shoulder. "We're sorry to see you go, Ellie. But we're so glad we got to know you here on the show."

"Thanks, Chris. I'll always cherish the time I spent here."

"Goodbye, Ellie," he said. And then she walked back to the line and through the French doors to pack.

Rochelle watched Grant as he made a final, rehearsed speech to end the episode. He looked so genuine and honest and vulnerable. Ellie's meltdown had clearly affected him. And it bothered Rochelle. Because it meant Grant wasn't as heartless as she had so desperately wanted to believe—and that he might very well have been a good man.

So does he deserve what I'm about to do to him?

Rochelle awoke to someone shaking her shoulder. She popped open one eye to see Maya standing over her looking frantic in her pajamas and pink silk robe. Her hair was disheveled and she had bags under her eyes. Bags that Rochelle had no doubt would disappear before morning. They always did. That was the magic that was Maya. "What is it? Is something wrong?" Rochelle said.

Maya sat on the bed, and Rochelle turned over fully to face her. "I figured it out," Maya said proudly.

Rochelle yawned and glanced at the clock. It was three o'clock in the morning, and Maya had just now decided she wanted to have a slumber party? "Figured what out?"

"All of it. You and Grant. You are the long-lost love he was talking about at the Friendship Ceremony last night. That first night when you dropped your wine glass? You didn't think he was your cousin. Nope, you recognized him. You two have a past."

Alarm surged through her as she sat up straight. "I don't know what you're talking about." But the words were thinly veiled through a layer of panic.

Maya smirked. "Sure you do. I see the way he looks at you. I see the way you look at him. You two were an item, and for some reason, Richie won't let either of you off the show. Tell me I'm wrong. Even if you do, I won't believe you."

Rochelle swallowed, looking long and hard at the woman sitting on her bed. She knew Maya was observant; she just didn't know she was a freaking sleuth. The real question was whether or not Maya was trustworthy. So far, she seemed to be decent. So far, she seemed to be the only contestant on this show, save Ellie, who was…well, normal. And right now, she didn't seem outraged or angry. In fact, she was acting as if she'd just won something. "What are you going to do?"

Maya crossed her arms. "Are you asking if I'm going to blow the whistle? That depends."

"On what?"

"On the circumstances. Tell me everything. Spill it, girl. And then we'll talk about me ratting you out."

What choice did she have? Maya had already figured it out—or at least, she'd figured *something* out. Instead of going to the other girls—or to Richie—she'd come to Rochelle first. That had to count for something, right?

And, all truth told, Rochelle wanted to tell Maya. Well, maybe not Maya exactly, but she wanted to tell *someone* what was going on, to be able to confide in someone about this catastrophe that had started off with good—sort of—intentions and had ended up a steamy hot mess. Maya seemed like as good a candidate as any.

Rochelle took in a galvanizing breath. This was happening. "Grant and I dated in college. It didn't work out." Only, she didn't stop there. She told Maya all of it, all the dirty details. The dinner, the breakup, Tiffany Freaking Wallace, the auditions for the show, the dire state of Helping Hands, and her new opportunity to take revenge. A full hour had passed before she stopped talking.

Maya had been a good listener. But now she appeared mortified. "Oh no," she said. "You can't take revenge on him."

That wasn't what Rochelle had been expecting to hear. "Did you miss the part where he sabotaged one of the happiest moments of my life by breaking up with me and shattering my freaking heart into a million jagged pieces?"

Maya placed her hand on Rochelle's. "But don't you see? You still care about him. You think you hate him, but girl, there's a fine line between love and hate. The fact that you still want revenge so badly tells me that you're not over him."

She blinked. Maybe confiding in Maya hadn't been such a great idea after all, especially if she was going to come up with such ridiculous theories. *But are these theories so ridiculous if I'd already considered them myself?* All she could muster was, "Be serious."

Maya shook her head, eyes full of sadness. "You've got a second chance here. Grant's available and interested in sorting it out."

"But I'm not interested." A lie, and she knew it.

Maya sighed. "On your one-on-one date, he said he was going to propose. But that you moved on to bigger and better things."

"Yeah, but he couldn't have been talking about me. I never would have left Grant for someone else."

"Not someone, some*thing*. Girl, he broke up with you because he didn't want to hold you back from law school!"

Rochelle's mouth gaped open. "He didn't say that. He said he was bored with me. And anyways, I was going to ask him to come with me, remember?"

Maya shook her head emphatically. "But you never did tell him that, did you?"

She blinked. "Well. No. I went back to tell him, though. And that's when I saw him with *her*." The memory of Tiffany's long legs flowing out of a short jean skirt as she sat on Grant's lap had her almost hyperventilating.

"Oh geez. Haven't you ever heard of a rebound?"

"Rebound! Who needs a rebound three hours after a breakup?"

"He thought he made sure you weren't coming back. To him, he had nothing else to lose. He had a ring, Rochelle. You don't think he would have gone with you?"

Rochelle felt on the verge of vomiting. *He had nothing else to lose.* "Oh my God. What if that's true?"

"That's a question only you can answer."

Oh no. Not this. Anything but this. What if Maya was right? Had she been so stubborn that she'd just let Grant throw things away without trying to fix it herself? *But I did go back. And he was with someone else. Doesn't that answer all these questions?* No, no it doesn't. She remembered when she'd moved to her new campus, she practically became a serial dater trying to forget Grant. She'd had at least twenty first dates that never evolved into anything else. Is that what happened with Grant, too?

She swallowed hard. Could it really be this simple? "So? What are you going to do?" she said. "About the show, I mean?" As in, was she completely screwed in every aspect of her life now?

Maya stood, looking down at her thoughtfully. "I'm not going to snitch, if that's what you're asking. Your secret is safe with me."

Rochelle exhaled in relief. "Thank you."

Hopefully none of the other contestants were as perceptive as Maya. She had to stay on the show at least long enough to get this resolved once and for all. *The question is: if Maya is right, what am I going to do about it?*

Chapter Eighteen

This was the week Grant had been dreading. With one-on-one dates, there would be a certain expectation that Grant would sleep with one or more of the women to "test their bedroom compatibility." Any of them would have qualified for a one-night stand in Grant's book. They were all attractive, successful women, after all. But he hadn't come on this show for a one-night stand.

He hadn't even come on this show to find love. He'd come here strictly to get revenge on Rochelle. Plus, he figured it couldn't hurt to be enticed by beautiful women, once he'd voted off the one who'd crushed his desire to ever pursue a serious relationship again.

But now he realized he'd always wanted a serious relationship—with Rochelle.

So there would be no testing bedroom compatibility with anyone other than her—and he had already squandered his chance with her on their one-on-one date. He hadn't even gotten the chance to touch her that night, because she'd walked away when dinner started to go well. It pained him that he'd forfeited the chance to seduce her, to remind her of what they could be together.

Still, he knew jumping into bed with her wasn't the immediate answer, although the tightness in his jeans just thinking about it said otherwise. Rochelle needed some gentle coaxing, some delicate care, a lot of nurturing—and to know that he was still the man she loved. He knew she'd loved him before. And somehow, he had to find a way to make her love him again.

In the meantime, he should find some more cooperative jeans...

Plus, a good excuse to keep them on tonight.

And that was why he was flagging down one of the camera crew at that very moment, a short man loading hard silver suitcases into the boat they'd be taking to the island today. "Excuse me," Grant said. "Can I use your cell phone? I need to get in a request to Richie."

"I can help you with that," Chris said from behind them. At any other time, his friend's ability to sneak up on him would have annoyed him, but this time it was a life saver.

"I've been craving some cookies," Grant said, aware that the short man loading the boat was giving him a curious look.

"We're about to leave for the island," Chris said dryly. "We don't have time to run to Grandma's house for some cookies."

"I'm certain you were in the room when Richie said that if I needed anything at all—"

"Does anyone have any cookies?" Chris yelled to the

crew surrounding them. All of them shrugged, none of them willing to make eye contact with Grant.

Grant shook his head. "I don't want just *any* cookies. I'm craving…a particular kind."

"Of course you are," Chris said, flexing his jaw. "What can we arrange for you, Grant? I want to make sure you're as comfortable as possible."

"I've been craving some Mrs. Field's Chocolate Chip Walnut cookies."

Chris blinked. "No, really. Be specific."

Obviously Chris wasn't catching on. Grant grabbed his arm and pulled him away from the spectators surrounding them. "Did you not hear me say that I need *walnut* cookies, jackass?"

Chris grinned. "I wondered how you were going to handle this. You're sure this is the route you want to take? I won't cut a second of the footage. All of America will see you as a leper."

Grant nodded hurriedly. "Get me a huge supply of them, will you? I want to have them all week."

"Do you at least have an EpiPen? The nearest hospital is about a hundred miles away."

"I've got it taken care of."

Chris shook his head. "At least this will make for some nice ratings."

"Screw you."

But Chris was already walking away.

Grant's first one-on-one date was with Cassandra, the twin who he'd reluctantly kept on the show despite her forwardness and aggression in pursuing him. Cassandra had been very open about her intentions up until this point, both on and off camera, giving him not-so-subtle hints about what she expected out of this evening. He was glad to get this one out of the way first.

The Dream Suite was located on a small private island in the tropics, and according to Richie, boasted a setting so romantic, he would have to beat the women off of him. Especially a woman like Cassandra.

Even now, as his boat turned in to dock at the small inlet of the island, he could see her walking along the beach and waving to him wildly. He fixed a smile on his face and inhaled slowly. Two minutes max, and he'd be at her mercy. He waited until well after the boat was securely tied to the pier before he disembarked; the cameraman next to him nudged him, motioning for him to get out of the boat so he could get the shot.

Cassandra's tiny yellow bikini barely kept everything in place as she ran down the dock and hurled herself at Grant. "Finally, we're alone!" she squealed.

"Finally," he breathed.

This is going to be a long night—and where are my cookies?

He'd warded off her kisses underneath the waterfall in the pool by asking about her work as a dolphin trainer. When she sat on his lap in the paddleboat, he'd pretended the weight imbalance would flip them over. And when she'd placed a hand on his leg and caressed her way up to his crotch at dinner, he'd faked a choking. A choking that required a member of the camera crew to administer the Heimlich. He was sure his ribs would be bruised for weeks, but the pain was well worth it.

Still, it had been an embarrassing, exhausting, unmanly day.

And none of it got him out of convening with Cassandra in the Dream Suite. Even now, he waited with the camera crew, standing there in his pajama pants like a little boy waiting for Santa. And for his walnut-infested cookies. Chris Asshat Legend had all but disappeared. Things did not bode well.

With nothing else to do but stand around, Grant and the camera crew watched the bathroom door, waiting for Cassandra to emerge from it. Richie had told Grant—and smiled while doing it—that the crew would film her entrance and his reaction to her, and then leave for the night so they could have privacy.

And Cassandra was more than prepared for the occasion. When she finally exited the bathroom, she wore a black leather-and-lace corset, a skimpier-than-most thong and the tallest platform sandals Grant had ever seen. In her hands, she cradled a leather whip, caressing it as though it were her firstborn. Someone in the crew behind him whistled, bringing a devious smile to Cassandra's face. "Are you ready for me, Grant?"

She strode across the room as if on the runway and took his face into her hands. Without warning, she pulled his mouth down on hers, pressing her body into him. Cassandra knew exactly what she was doing. It was a kiss meant to se-duce—a kiss he would have appreciated about three months ago before Rochelle was ushered back into his life. But now it was no use. He had a very singular craving, and Cassandra was not it. Gently, he took her shoulders and pushed her back, offering her what he hoped looked like a pleased grin.

"We have all night," he said. "No need to rush." He took her hand and brushed a kiss on it for reassurance, but she pursed her lips.

"You're right," she said. "But we can go slow later. Right now I want those lips anywhere but my hand."

Jesus, he needed to put a stop to this—and now. Desper-ately, he skimmed the room, looking for the food and drink cart Chris had told him would be in there. It was nowhere to be found. How difficult could it possibly have been to find walnut cookies? Every convenience store with a snack aisle had them. Surely the people of the tropics enjoyed the deca-dence of cookies now again?

Grant jerked his head away as Cassandra dove in again. He held her at arms' length, contemplating his next move. "Before we do this, I need to tell you something," he said, forcing himself to look into her eyes. But he had nothing. What could he possibly say to this woman that would turn her off? What could be better than bulbous welts sprouting all over his face and body?

Chris Schnartz-Legend was a dead man. He'd had one job, to fetch some cookies, and he'd utterly failed at it.

One.

Job.

"Yes, Grant?" Cassandra's smile was filled with confi-dence, as though she expected him to confess his undying love, or at the very least, his unquenchable desire for her.

"I tried to find a way to tell you all day, but there never seemed to be a good time." Maybe he could tell her that he's a virgin. Or that he was saving himself for marriage. But a woman like Cassandra would likely find his innocence a thrilling conquest. She'd brought a leather whip to the Dream Suite, for God's sake.

"I thought you were acting shy," she laughed seductively. "But don't worry. By the end of the night, neither of us will have anything to be shy about anymore."

"Cassandra—"

"Now's not the time for talking, Grant." She slapped the whip against her palm, then pulled him in for another kiss, which he was barely able to dodge. The camera rolled as Grant nearly threw himself across the room, away from her and her flailing weapon. He picked up a frilly pillow from the bed and tucked it into folded arms in front of him. As if that would protect him.

Why isn't the camera crew leaving? Can't they just do me this one favor? But no, frame by frame, they continued to film his humiliation.

"You've filmed the entrance and reaction," Grant said quietly to them. "Cassandra and I are at least entitled to *some* privacy, aren't we?" That's when he noticed that Chris had arrived. He exchanged glances with his friend. Chris stepped forward, an amused look on his face. *I'm going to strangle that bastard.*

"We're going to keep the cameras rolling a while," Chris said. "It can be edited later. Everything can be edited later."

Son of a—

"Is this a game?" Cassandra asked, undeterred. She

backed Grant up to the space of wall beside the bed. "I like games. Am I the hunter, or the prey?" She traced a finger down his bare chest, then tried to tug the pillow from his grasp.

Definitely the hunter. He adjusted the pillow back in place, pushing her away—this time less gently. "Cassandra, I'm serious. We need to talk."

She gave him the poutiest of faces. "You're going to make me beg?"

"No," he said, clearing his throat. Again, he gave the crew a warning glance. *Get out!* he wanted to scream. Flustered, he ran a hand through his hair.

Cassandra had already made her way back to him. She reached out and placed a hand on his bicep, giving it a gentle squeeze. He'd never felt so dirty in his whole life. He tried to push past her, but she grabbed his wrist. "I love role play," she murmured.

She wouldn't be stopped.

The camera crew wouldn't leave.

Chris wouldn't forfeit the cookies.

He had no choice. "Cassandra—" he said. But as he took another step back, he bumped into something. Something that had a familiar laugh. He whirled around to face Chris, who stood there grinning like an idiot.

"I believe you requested dessert, before uh, dessert," he said. He offered Grant a plastic bag with a bow on it. A plastic bag filled with cookies. "Sorry it took so long. We had to bake them fresh."

Grant's exhale could be heard in the next room as he snatched the bag from his friend and tore it open like a man who hadn't eaten for days. "We should have some cookies," he told Cassandra, who eyed him like a man who hadn't bathed in days. He pulled out the largest one and shoved it in his mouth.

Cassandra gave him a venomous look. "*Cookies*? That couldn't have waited?"

"Cookies are sort of my fetish," Grant said, his insides unfurling with relief. "They really get me in the mood." Behind him, Chris snorted. "I'd love to see what you look like wearing only these cookies."

She gave him a mischievous smile. "You won't have an appetite for cookies once I get out of these clothes."

"I'll bet," he said shoving another one in his mouth. He tasted the glorious bits of walnut straightaway, willing the little life-saving and life-threatening tidbits into his bloodstream.

Cassandra turned a glare on Chris. "You can go now. I'm going to make sure none of this is suitable for family television."

To get things moving faster, Grant scratched at his neck and face, trying to disturb the skin there. His skin didn't disappoint him but responded almost instantly; he felt the scratches raising up, turning into bumps that would soon become inflamed ridges all over him. His bottom lip swelled, and heat filled his cheeks. Even the lobes of his ears began to itch. Not a moment too soon, either.

Cassandra's smiled faded to a scowl. "Grant, your face. You've got bumps all over it."

He held up his arms and hands for her to see the rash there, as well. Repulsed, she stepped away from him. Grant heard Chris smother a laugh.

There would be no sex tonight, of that Grant was

positive. Reveling in the prickly feel of new blisters developing on his skin, he offered the plastic bag to Cassandra. "You sure you don't want some?" He took care to chew with his mouth open. More than a few crumbs escaped his lips. It was a gross display, and he was proud of it.

Cassandra sat on the bed and sighed. "I'm not hungry. Maybe we could just…talk."

Success.

Chapter Nineteen

Rochelle let herself into Richie's office unannounced. She strode to his desk and pressed her palms into the edge of it. His chair was turned away from her, facing the bookshelf.

"I'm not going," she said to the back of Richie's desk chair.

"Oh, but you are," he answered cheerfully without turning around.

"The rules state that the bachelor comes home with me to meet my family. I don't *have* a family. Unless we're supposed to visit the penitentiary?" She shouldn't have offered that. Knowing Richie, he'd take her up on it, and they'd have a picnic in the yard with her worthless father, surrounded by guards with big guns and little patience.

He swirled around, mirth in his eyes. "Now that's a thought, isn't it?"

Rochelle nearly snarled. "I should be disqualified during

home visits."

"Even orphans get a chance to seduce the bachelor during homecoming week, my dear. Otherwise that would be discrimination, wouldn't it?"

"And who's going to bring that up? Me?"

But Richie ignored her. "We've arranged for *you* to visit *his* family."

She threw her hands up in frustration. "I've already met his family, Richie, and trust me, the reunion won't be pretty." The thought of going back to that town, of reliving her last days there, of reliving memories of an actual happy time of her life...could be very dangerous.

She'd already admitted to herself that despite her best efforts to deny it, she still had feelings for Grant. Some of them were murderous feelings. But some of them were... sentimental. She'd suffered through all the days he'd spent in the Dream Suite with the other contestants, trying to keep images of him in bed with the other women out of her head. Maya had reassured her that their night together had been spent making sure Grant's throat didn't close up—some freak allergic reaction—but what about the other women? Had he taken advantage of the circumstances? Had he put his hands on them?

God, she wished she didn't care. But she could no longer deny that he still held a piece of her heart that no man would ever have access to again. And it was a bigger piece than she cared to admit.

She just couldn't let him back in, though. She wouldn't. Maybe he'd had good intentions, but he'd broken her heart without giving her a chance to explain her plans. He'd taken matters into his own hands and not given her a choice. She couldn't let him get that close to her again. She couldn't expose herself to him.

Could she?

"His family won't have me," she said, changing tactics. "I almost burned their house down." They hadn't had any hard feelings about that at the time, but Richie didn't need to know that.

"Mrs. Drake has already consented to keep your secret a secret," he said with glee. "She's actually looking forward to seeing you again."

Rochelle pinched the bridge of her nose. "Richie. Please."

"We made a deal, Rochelle. A solid deal. Are you backing out now that you've come so far?" He leaned forward, concern etched into his brow. "Wait a minute. Are you falling in love with Grant again?"

"What? No!"

"The cameras don't lie. I saw how you were looking at him when he let Ellie go."

"It was a nice thing to do. I would have been pleased with anyone who did that. Grant's not special." Still, her cheeks felt warm underneath the accusation. When Grant had handed Ellie that donation check, he'd given her a glimpse of what he used to be…and apparently what he still was.

"Oh, but he is, isn't he, Rochelle? Otherwise you wouldn't have a problem going to visit his family—being with him in his most intimate environment. I never thought a woman like you would be afraid of a man."

Richie was more perceptive than Rochelle had given him credit for. *Crap.* "I'm not afraid of Grant. And I'm not falling for your stupid mind-games. If I don't want to reunite with his family, I don't have to, contractually."

"Incorrect."

"Richie—"

"Oh enough!" He stood abruptly. Rochelle wasn't aware he could actually move with any sort of startling speed. "You're going, or the deal's off."

"You can't do that."

"Technically, we put nothing in writing. As an attorney, you should know how detrimental that would be to your case, were you to pursue it."

She pressed her lips together, wanting to—needing to—slap the smile off his smug face. Of course, she knew she was screwed without documentation. And she recognized that this tactic of hers was obviously not working. She crossed her arms. "You don't understand, Richie. His family will ruin it. They won't keep their mouths shut about our past relationship. Oh, they'll promise you the moon and they'll have the best of intentions to give it to you. But they're just not *capable* of silence. You're really letting all his siblings on the show? Besides, Grant's mother is the town gossip queen. She's the owner of the beauty salon, for God's sake. If you really wanted to keep it a secret and not undermine *your own show*, you wouldn't take that risk. You may have already ruined it by telling them I'm even here." She snorted. "They'll probably put up a 'Welcome Home Rochelle' banner at city hall. How will you explain that to your staff?"

Though Grant's mother *did* run the town beauty salon, she was the opposite of a gossip queen. She was so unconcerned with idle chitchat that she even forgot to impart important details at vital times. She once had a car accident, totaling the family's only vehicle and fracturing her arm, and forgot to tell Grant's stepdad until it was time to pick him up from the airport after his business trip. She'd chafed at the thought of bothering him with the news until he got back.

If anything, Sharon Drake was an exceptional listener and a superb keeper of secrets. She could probably have been an international spy and her family and closest friends would never have known it. Rochelle recalled a time when the only person she could really confide in was Sharon. She'd even told her what had happened with Grant at dinner that night. Sharon had been certain she'd misinterpreted the situation. That's when Rochelle had realized she could never confide in Sharon again. Not when she thought her son could do no wrong. So, in one fell swoop, she'd lost the love of her life and the mother that she'd never really had.

Richie's smile vanished, replaced by a grimace of self-doubt. "Grant said his mother was retired. And his siblings won't be there. Even I would never take a risk like that."

His siblings wouldn't be there. Rochelle was almost disappointed. How empty the house must feel to Sharon with all her babies gone. But that wasn't the point. "Oh, his mother is retired all right. From the Air Force. Now she dresses hair to pass the time. She gets paid in rumors." Lies, all of it. But she had to get out of this home visit. It could be detrimental to her plan to not fall in love with Grant Drake. Again.

Now it was Richie's turn to pinch the bridge of his nose. He let out a low growl. "That woman swore to me she wouldn't tell a soul."

Rochelle clicked her tongue. "You'd be a fool to believe that."

He tapped his fingers on his desk as he contemplated.

After a while, he looked up, a satisfied grin tugging at his lips. "You know what I think, Rochelle Ransom? I think I'd be a fool to believe *you*. If you turn out to be right, and the whole thing crumbles to ashes, I'll still pay you for our deal. But my instincts say otherwise, and my instincts are never wrong. You're going. End of discussion."

Crap.

Chapter Twenty

Grant settled into his first class seat, unable to appreciate the fact that he had the entire row to himself for the duration of the flight. The word "hellish" had been invented for the last four days Grant had endured spending time with the families of the contestants, and no amount of free liquor or eager attentiveness from the flight attendants could make up for it. The two days he'd spent at each contestant's home felt like a lifetime of awkward situations and painful conversation—especially at Cassandra's house in Orlando.

The first day had gone fairly well when she'd introduced him to all her colleagues at the aquarium where she worked as a dolphin trainer. Thank God the most seductive thing she changed into was a wetsuit this time. But when it came time to meet the family—and be reunited with her twin sister who he'd scorned earlier on the show—well, the word "pandemonium" had been invented for that hour of insanity.

He was greeted at the front door with a slap to the face

from Cassandra and Stephanie's mother, who'd promptly scolded him for "treating my girls unequally." Richie had insisted that Stephanie attend the family dinner that night to increase the tension, and Chris didn't stop the cameras from rolling until Grant's lap was fully drenched in gravy and his head pummeled with every last piece of cornbread on the table.

His meeting with the family of Jacquelyn, the chef, didn't go much better, though on the plus side, he hadn't been bombarded with food. Her father was a widower and a retired army drill sergeant, who ran his household like a war bunker. As soon as he arrived, Grant was given an itinerary for the next two days, broken down into fifteen-minute intervals. His genitals were also threatened in the event that they came near the sergeant's daughter during his visit. Jacquelyn prepared delicious meals for the three of them, but Grant's appetite was non-existent. He'd been too busy pondering how he would subdue the old sergeant without hurting him or losing his own testicles in the process.

Why are my testicles always in danger on this show?

To say the least, he was hoping—praying even—to get some much-needed sleep on the flight to see Maya's family in Mississippi. She would be waiting at the airport when he arrived, and with any kind of luck, her family would be as normal as she was. That was his last thought as he dozed off without drinking the screwdriver he'd ordered.

Maya waited for him by baggage claim B, wielding a gorgeous, genuine smile and a mason jar of what appeared to be sweet tea for him. She kissed him on the cheek and handed him the glass, which he gratefully accepted. "Welcome to the South," she said. "My father has the car pulled around to pick us up."

Grant smiled, taking a sip from the jar. "You're as sweet as this tea."

"You must be exhausted. Do you need me to carry anything for you?"

He sighed in relief. Finally. Normalcy. Hospitality. Manners. He was reminded again of why he liked Maya so much. "No, thanks. Let me get my bags; I don't want to keep your father waiting."

"He's anxious to meet you." She hesitated. "He...thinks this whole dating show is a scam. So he'll probably give you the third degree. Try not to be offended, okay?"

Great, he thought as he retrieved his luggage from the belt.

When they got to the car, a clean high-end SUV, Maya's father immediately extended his hand. He was a tall black man, with wise eyes and gray-tinged hair, but his wrinkles revealed smile lines instead of those caused by habitual frowns. He seemed nervous about the camera crew standing a few feet from them, filming everything. Grant hardly noticed them anymore. How different his life had become.

"Hi there, Grant," her father said. "I'm James Atmore. Friends call me Jimbo. You can, too, I suppose."

"The pleasure is mine, sir," Grant said, shaking his hand.

"Jimbo," he corrected. "Sir is for the British and the uppity." He opened the hatch of the SUV and without asking, grabbed Grant's luggage and placed it neatly inside. "I hope you didn't eat during your layover; we've got the best barbecue on this side of the state line waiting for you at the house."

"Dad!" Maya said, exasperated. "That was supposed to be a surprise!"

Grant's stomach rumbled. He hadn't enjoyed a proper, peaceful meal in days. Not that he could have eaten, anyway, what with all the chaos whirling around him. "That sounds amazing, sir—Jimbo."

The older man smiled. "Sir Jimbo. I could get used to that."

Maya took Grant's hand and led him to the backseat. After they'd settled and were on the road, she leaned toward him. "I know it's wrong to ask," she said, "but I'm dying to know how the other visits went. Are you allowed to tell me?"

He sighed. "Technically, no. But frankly, they were catastrophic."

She giggled. "I can't wait to watch the episodes."

"Scandalous," he laughed.

The Atmore house was situated on a huge plot of land surrounded by aged trees burdened with hanging moss swaying lazily in the breeze. It was an older home, with a wrap-around porch on both stories and a tire swing tied to the oak tree closest to the house. Grant could imagine a much younger Maya laughing and swinging without a care in the world. Even now, she smiled and talked with ease, as if life itself was her best friend.

Someone would kill to wake up to a smile like that every day. Too bad the smile he'd longed for hadn't made a true appearance since their one-on-one date. What he wouldn't give for a genuine smile from Rochelle.

But the smile Maya gave him then brought him back to

reality. She nodded past him, toward property.

Behind the house, a small line of smoke trailed into the sky and suddenly a whiff of lilacs and smoked meat attacked his senses. Jimbo looked at him in the rearview mirror and chuckled. "You look like a starved cat in a tuna cannery. Look now, I know my pulled pork will be the best thing you ever tasted, but if you don't pay Granny a compliment on her potato salad, there'll be hell to pay in a lump sum."

Grant smiled. "You can count on me for at least two big helpings of it."

Jimbo nodded. "You just might survive today, son."

And that was when the nerves set in. They dissolved only after Grant had met more than fifty of Maya's aunts, uncles, cousins, neighbors, and her only living Granny. The affair was sprawled out over the backyard with checkered tablecloth picnic tables, lawn chairs in between, and two big grills off to the side. To the right was what looked like a fierce horseshoe match, and to the left were at least ten children all in different stages of hula-hooping. The scene was something out of a family movie. Grant couldn't help but feel charmed.

Plus, everyone seemed to actually get along. Not once had a piece of cornbread been hurled at an unsuspecting victim. *Surely the world is coming to an end*, he thought as he took his first bite of potato salad, careful to arrange his expression into delight despite the bitterness that deluged his mouth. He was well aware that Granny watched him from two picnic tables over. He resisted the urge to grab his sweet tea and unload a mouthful of potato backwash into it. *Why did I have to take such a big bite?*

Even Maya seemed surprised at his bold move.

"My God," Grant told Maya loudly. "This has got to be the best potato salad I've ever tasted."

The entire gathering grew silent, still. The loud clink of one of the horseshoes hitting the stake resounded through the back yard, calling attention to the sudden lull in conversation. Granny was giving him a sharp look of disapproval. Grant had the inexplicable urge to hide under the table. But the table would have hidden him no better than the tea would have hidden a load of backwash.

Then suddenly, Granny erupted into laughter, guffawing so hard Grant was sure she was going to spit out her dentures. It took only seconds for everyone else to join her. Someone behind him spit out their drink. One of Maya's neighbors clutched her stomach as if she'd gone into labor. What was the matter with these people? *So much for normal.*

A full minute passed before Jimbo could catch his breath. He grasped Grant's shoulder, leaning on him for support. Jimbo was heavier than he looked. "That's radish dressing, son. Granny's potato salad is on that table over yonder. But you passed the test anyway."

Blood rushed to Grant's face. Radish dressing. *There's such a thing as radish dressing?* "Test?"

"You're polite and respectful. I won't have my daughter dating a heathen."

"But that doesn't get you out of eating my potato salad, young man," Granny called out, pointing a shaking finger at him. Only now her eyes held a certain twinkle. One Grant hadn't noticed before.

After the last of the guests had left and the backyard was a reasonable degree of untidy , Maya took Grant's hand. This was the second time she'd done it today; on the show, she was never this bold. Sure she hugged him a few times at some of the Friendship Ceremonies, but the embraces were quick and friendly. Nothing as intimate as holding hands. She was even caressing his hand with her thumb as they walked.

She's definitely in her element here.

Together they hopped into an old Ford pickup; the ever-present camera crew loaded up in the back. Maya drove them down a moonlit dirt road. "This was my first car. Can you believe that man gave me something with no power steering?"

"Sounds like something my mom would do."

"My mom left us when I was three years old. In case you were wondering." She said it as if confessing something. As if her mother leaving was the fault of a three-year-old child.

"I hope you don't expect me to feel sorry for you," he said playfully. "I had to put up with my mother, so you'll get no sympathy from me."

Maya laughed. If he'd been with one of the other contestants, he would have been worried she'd take that the wrong way. He should have known better with Maya.

"This would be a lot more romantic without the boys," she whispered, nodding toward the truck bed.

Grant considered that both good and bad. Good, because if things got intimate with Maya, he'd have to find a way out of it before he ruined his chances with Rochelle. He was hoping that Maya would be shy in front of the camera, the lady he thought she was—who did not want to arm Chris with an episode of PDA.

Bad, because he'd like to get to know Maya better, and she wouldn't likely open up to him in front of the camera, PDA or not. He could tell she would make an excellent friend, but an overly romantic setting would give her the wrong idea.

Maya backed the truck up to the edge of a creek that rushed noisily past them and glistened in the moonlight. She motioned for the crew to hop out. As the crew set up a few feet away, Maya retrieved a fuzzy blanket from the toolbox in the back and spread it out over the bed of the truck. Patting the space beside her, she smiled up at Grant. "How about some star-gazing?"

A loud clank resounded in the night, followed by a whispered expletive. Grant shook his head. "You're right. This would be more romantic without them. A chicken coop would be more romantic." Thank God. He settled next to her and they laid back. The evening was cloudless and the stars weren't shy, sparkling above them like a faraway city in the sky.

Chris leaned his forearms on the side of the truck. "Don't talk about anything important until we're rolling."

Grant rolled his eyes. "How long will that be, you think?"

"About five minutes."

They stayed there in silent obedience, Grant because he didn't know what to say, and Maya—he got the distinct feeling that Maya stayed mum because she was a stringent rule-follower. Since the beginning of *Luring Love*, she'd never crossed boundaries, disobeyed any orders, or talked out of line. She'd been a perfect lady.

If only he wanted a perfect lady.

"We're on," Chris announced.

Grant took in a deep breath. *Here we go again*. It wasn't that he wasn't fond of Maya. She had the most to offer out of any of the contestants in the way of interesting and friendly conversation. What was more, he felt relaxed around her. Maya seemed like a real person, instead of just a representation she was trying to put forward.

It was just that these uptight, forced dates had been awkward at best and cataclysmic most of the time. Of course, if everyone had behaved themselves, the ratings would have plummeted and the show would flop. So Richie had strategically picked contestants with a dramatic flair—to put it mildly. Grant was just grateful that Richie threw in a normal one, too.

"It was the cookies, wasn't it?" Maya said suddenly.

"What do you mean?" he said, trying to swallow the surprise in his voice. She really was much bolder out here in her world, even with the cameras rolling.

"You ate the cookies in order to have an allergic reaction."

Grant wondered how miserably he was failing at appearing innocent. Maya had been the best sport about his hives. Nurse that she was, she had the swelling down in no time. He'd felt bad about even pulling that stunt on her. But it had to be done. "Why would I do that?"

"To get out of sleeping with someone."

"That's...an interesting strategy."

"Oh, come on. Let's be honest here." She turned to her side and rested her head on her arm, looking at him with thoughtful eyes. "The girls have all been talking about your long-lost love, and how you might not be over her. You babbled on about her at the Friendship Ceremony, Grant."

"Babbled?"

She shrugged. "None of us want to hear about another girl. Even me."

"Go on."

"So you ate those cookies, knowing the result would turn everyone off from…being intimate with you."

Grant cocked his head. Maya was way too observant. "Did it turn you off?"

"Yes." *And she was painfully honest.*

"What if it wasn't my idea? What if the show insisted on it for ratings and such?" He heard Chris suck in a breath and wondered if that bit would be cut in editing.

"If you hadn't admitted to being in love with someone else, I might believe you. But sex sells, everyone knows that."

Chris coughed. Loudly. This part was definitely not making it to air.

Grant sighed in surrender. "You know, just because I'm still in love with someone doesn't mean I haven't slept with anyone since her." He wasn't sure if he was trying to deny that he'd purposely induced his allergy, or if he was worried about coming off as a love-struck prude. On both counts, he sounded a little desperate. He resisted the urge to run a hand through his hair.

"I didn't say that, did I?" she said.

"I guess I'm not exactly sure what you're saying." *Or what I'm saying.*

She laughed. "I'm just saying that it's okay if you don't want to sleep with all of us — or any of us. It doesn't make you weird. It makes you a gentleman. And anyways, I've used that same excuse before. The allergy, I mean. I'm allergic to latex."

He grinned, turning on his side too. "Be serious." *A*

nurse allergic to latex?

She shrugged, giggling. "I break out like you do. It's gotten me out of work a few times, and once, out of a blind date. It was great."

"So, do the other contestants think I purposely caused an allergic reaction, too?" Had she told anyone else her theory? Had she told Rochelle?

"Some are suspicious, I think."

"Are you offended?"

"There's not much to be offended about, is there? It means you're not one to take advantage of a woman, even under tempting circumstances. You also did it in such a way that none of us felt like we were being rejected. That's makes you a gentleman. And if you're still caught up on a certain someone…Well, that makes you incredibly dreamy."

Dreamy. If only she knew the sour details. If only she knew it was Rochelle he was still in love with. "So is this gameplay? You stand back and observe everyone, then confront them with brutal honesty and demand to know their secrets? Should I expect blackmail next?"

She tilted her head. "When I auditioned for the show, I told myself that I wouldn't play the game. I would be myself, and if you liked me, you liked me, and if you didn't, it wasn't meant to be. But then I saw how great you are. And I wanted to make all the other girls go away, so you would only see me. So yes, I watched them. I watched what they were doing, which was essentially throwing themselves at you. Or calling attention to themselves. And I decided that the best way to stand out was to *not* stand out." She paused. "But the thing is, if you're still in love with someone else, you need to go after her."

Grant swallowed. The conversation was taking a more intimate turn than he'd expected. He was now accepting love advice from a contestant he was supposed to be wooing on camera. Was Maya really that selfless? "And how do you propose I do that? I'm stuck on this show."

She gave him a thoughtful look. "You know what I think? I think that no one is ever really stuck. You could use this show to get her back. You declared on national television that you were still in love with her, right? That's no small thing. I think you shouldn't give up trying if you love her that much. Convince her that she should leave the past in the past."

"What? Like send her coded messages through the show?" Wasn't that what he'd already been doing? But Rochelle seemed to reject every attempt, every step he took. He doubted a banner in the sky would get through to her at this point.

She raised a brow. "Try harder." And that was that. She simply put her head back on the blanket and watched the stars, leaving Grant the space to dissect what she'd said — and if any of her advice was humanly possible.

Convince the woman he loved to leave the past in the past. It sounded simple enough. But with Rochelle, nothing was ever uncomplicated. And being in front of a camera crew all the time didn't help. Still, she hadn't quit *Luring Love* yet. For whatever reason, she was still there holding on to whatever Richie had bribed her with.

He'd be a fool if he didn't use every opportunity to pursue her while he had the chance — something he already knew. But had he really done *all* he could?

Chapter Twenty-One

As the limo came to a stop on Main Street, Rochelle could hardly believe her eyes. Her wholesome hometown had turned into a commercial oasis. Maggie's Diner had been replaced with a fast food restaurant. The little bookstore on the corner, where she used to buy her used university textbooks, was now a fancy-schmancy coffee shop. There was even a yoga studio where Mr. Holcomb's watch repair shop used to be down the street, for God's sake.

Was nothing sacred in the world anymore?

This used to be a sleepy little town that only awoke on Friday nights for those going to the high school football game. If the season was over, for those old enough to drink or spry enough to dance. And Sunday mornings, for those who were repentant enough for their Friday night shenanigans to attend church.

When the limo passed Sharon Drake's beauty salon— still intact and unchanged, right down to the faded lettering on the windows—Rochelle breathed a sigh of relief.

If Sharon Drake had sold out, Rochelle just might have cried.

And I thought I hated this town. When what I truly hated was that Grant had shattered my dreams of being happy here.

Grant.

She was back in town to spend two full days with the man who'd destroyed her heart and hopes and fanciful dreams of taking his last name—dreams that, come to find out, hadn't been so fanciful at all. He'd said he'd bought a ring. He'd said he was going to ask her to marry him. For about five seconds, she'd been prepared to exact revenge on Grant. Make him fall for her again, then break his heart into unrecognizable remnants that he'd never be able to put back together. But deep down, she knew she couldn't do it.

Am I caving? And if so, to what exactly? To the fact that Grant might still have feelings for me? Do I even care?

There had been a time when she'd known the answers to these questions. A time when they would not even have been viable questions to ask. But that was before her conversation with Maya. That was when she thought with her mind, instead of with her heart. That was when her heart was no longer qualified to make decisions for her, having been splintered into fragments.

Before she auditioned for the show, she'd admitted to herself that her heart had somehow welded itself whole again, even if it was still badly scarred. That if, for some unlikely reason, she actually *liked* the bachelor and the prize money became secondary in the competition, she could handle it if he rejected her—and she could handle a relationship if he didn't.

But she had never imagined that the bachelor would be Grant Drake. She never dreamed she would have to reexamine what had happened all those years ago—and that she just might have been able to feel something other than hatred for him. Yet, it had happened. And she had yet to deal with it.

It wasn't even a question of what Grant deserved. It was a question of what *she* deserved. And did she deserve to be happy?

She'd already accepted that Tiffany had been Grant's rebound. Yes, it was a mere three hours after their breakup, but how could she really fault him? She'd done virtually the same thing as soon as she left town. Maybe she would have done the same thing if she hadn't been busy packing her stuff to get out of the state.

Rochelle gasped as she realized where they were. Somehow, someway, the limo was already pulling into the long driveway of Grant's parents' house. Rochelle straightened her shoulders, forcing her chin upward. It was show time.

The hedges of neatly trimmed azalea bushes were bigger than she remembered, and there were what appeared to be Christmas lights draped all over them, even though it was almost the end of July. It must be incredibly breathtaking to walk this little sparkling avenue at night—she hoped she wouldn't be subjected to it while she visited. Being here again already had her nerves rampaging; she didn't need any romantic walks in an enchanted driveway to confuse her further.

Every few yards, they passed full birdfeeders nailed to white fence posts—proof of Sharon's desire to spend more time with nature than with people. The upkeep on these birdfeeders, keeping them full and clean and in repair, was a time-consuming task, one that Sharon loved doing. It was a chore she never delegated to any of her children, one that she'd always insisted on doing herself, and alone at that.

The birdfeeders and their patrons kept Sharon Drake sane.

The car stopped. The driver got out, opened the door for her, and offered a hand to exit the car. As soon as she was on her feet, she saw Grant standing on the front porch, arms crossed. His expression was unreadable, as she hoped her own was. However, his mother, who stood beside him, could barely restrain her excitement.

Rochelle felt another small crack in the wall she'd put up around herself. This was going to be difficult. She hadn't spoken to Sharon Drake since she'd left town. Sharon had been one of her closest friends, but speaking to her, hearing a voice and a Southern accent that sounded so much like Grant's… It would have been like salting a laceration on her heart. She simply couldn't do it.

Sharon stepped down from the porch, and Chris Legend appeared from God only knew where. "Hold on, Mrs. Drake. We're almost set up," he said, sounding more exasperated than usual.

She rolled her eyes. "You have to film *everything*?"

Rochelle felt a smirk coming on. She knew Chris would want to film her arrival, so she'd stayed put—and hopefully outwardly impassive. But Grant's mother wasn't used to having every blink documented for national television—and she wasn't used to taking orders from Chris Schnartz, a boy she practically raised as her own. He was a constant fixture in their household all through his childhood and got punished with Grant and the rest of his siblings when he strayed from good behavior.

What's more, Sharon was a private person. Private people sometimes lost their tactfulness. No doubt Sharon had already laid down the law, or at the very least some basic rules for Chris and his crew to follow; it would explain his annoyance now.

"As I said before, we're working as quickly as we can," Chris replied in a clipped tone. He disappeared to the side of the house, where Rochelle now heard the banter and exchanges of the mobile film crew.

Sharon gave her a scowl. "I don't know how you kids have put up with such nonsense."

"It hasn't been easy," Rochelle said.

"Hasn't it?" Grant said.

He means to point out to his mother how I've been acting on the show. By his lack of reaction these past weeks, she'd thought he'd barely even noticed anymore. Then again, at dinner during their one-on-one date, he had admitted he was on the lookout for her antics. Now he seemed hell-bent on exposing her to his family.

Snitches get stitches, she told him with her eyes.

Her stomach dropped as a realization struck her: She wouldn't have acted that way if her mind had been in charge. In fact, she'd been acting *out* of her mind the entire time. It had been her heart all along calling the shots. She'd only fooled herself into believing it was for Helping Hands. The truth was, she wanted to see how this would play out from the moment she saw Grant.

And not just because of her competitive nature. Deep down, she wanted to see *him*. Staying on the show was the only way she could do it. Richie's offer to double the prize money was convenient, of course. And it had quieted the indecision welling up inside her as she sat next to Grant in Richie's grand office, arguing about whether or not she'd stay on the show.

Every instinct screamed that she wasn't ready for this, for what this home visit would do to her. She wanted to slide back into the limo and tell the driver to take her to the airport where she could book a flight back to her cozy little city apartment where Grant had never existed except when he'd occasionally haunted her dreams. To stop looking at Grant right now, stop holding his gaze, stop noticing the way his stature was rigid with tension and his eyes were more combative than she'd ever seen them.

This is a game I had no business playing. And she was going to lose, no matter what she did. If she tried to win Grant back, and succeeded, it could only be a matter of time before he betrayed her again. If she walked away right now, she'd lose all the money for Helping Hands, and possibly the last chance she'd have with the only man who had ever been able to triple her heart rate.

Oh yes, she was going to lose. She saw that now. The only control she had at this point was what, exactly, she lost.

Sure that she wore her emotions on her face, Rochelle offered Grant a weak smile. "I did have the jitters the first few weeks. But I think I've adjusted now."

This answer threw him off, she could tell. And why wouldn't it? He was probably expecting something barbed and laced with arsenic to come out of her mouth. He cleared his throat then turned his attention to Chris, who stood at the corner of the house watching them both.

"You ready yet?" Grant said gruffly.

"Are you?" Chris countered.

They exchanged meaningful glares rife with testosterone. Rochelle couldn't hear what Grant muttered after that, but it was interrupted with "We're rolling!"

Sharon took the last two steps off the porch and Rochelle met her halfway for a full embrace. She wondered how America would react to this kind of intimate greeting between two people who were supposed to be perfect strangers—and she didn't really care. This was reality TV to everyone else; to her, it was now just plain reality. An all-new reality she intended to grab and run with.

Sharon gave her a last squeeze and turned them both to face Grant. "Welcome to our home," she said.

"Thank you," Rochelle replied, freshly amused with this scenario.

Even Grant seemed to appreciate the irony. The corner of his mouth rose just a bit. "Yes," he said. "Welcome to the circus."

Rochelle plucked the blackberry from the bush, weighing its plumpness in the palm of her hand. "I'm tempted to eat this one. Sharon, surely your cobbler can go without this one blackberry?"

Sharon puckered her lips. "I suppose it could."

Grant poked his head around the other side of the bush, a smirk etched into his expression. Rochelle suppressed a giggle. Sharon's reason for accompanying them to pick the blackberries was about more than just the company. She used to hate when Rochelle and Grant would return with half a basket or worse, none at all. Sure, she wanted to see Rochelle and visit with her son, but she also wanted a cobbler bursting with berries to present to the table on national television this evening. Baking was Sharon's one vanity.

"Grant, you already ate three. If you eat another, I'll swat you in front of all these cameras and your girlfriend here."

A chuckle waved through the crew. Chris may not have liked Sharon commandeering his show, but the rest of them had taken to her. In the three hours they'd been here, she'd offered them all tea and lemon cake and made sure they all had sunscreen on before traipsing out in the vast backyard—even though most of it was shaded with mature pine trees.

Grant popped another one in his mouth and winked at Rochelle. She turned around before she allowed the smile to reach her lips. From beside the camera, Chris gave her an ironic look. He was still the only one on the entire crew who knew what was really happening here. Maybe he thought she was giving up. Maybe he thought she was up to something.

Maybe he should mind his business and do his job, which, last time she checked, was hosting and directing. After all, he didn't get paid to do extra things like judge people, so why bother himself with it?

Still, she felt the blood warm her cheeks and hoped the cameras made it seem as if she was simply flushed on a hot July day. It bothered her that Chris knew why she'd been acting the way she had. And if she wasn't acting that way anymore, what was he to assume? What was *she* to assume?

But didn't I already make the decision that I'm going after Grant?

She looked up in time to see Grant give his mother a peck on the cheek before dumping the contents of his basket into hers. He wrapped his arm around her and she laughed. Sharon had missed her son. *That makes two of us.*

When he met her gaze, a fire settled in her stomach.

"I think I've got enough for a good-sized cobbler," Sharon announced. "Why don't you two get cleaned up and rested before supper?"

A shower. A nap. A sigh escaped her. "That sounds exquisite."

Rochelle was first to the back door and kicked off her shoes at the entryway just as she had done countless time before. Chris cleared his throat. *Oh. I'm not supposed to know to do that.*

She wondered if not following house rules—and therefore suffering the wrath of Sharon—would be a better alternative than simply doing what she liked and letting Chris worry about editing it out later. She decided the matter with a smile as she opened the cabinet in the utility room to retrieve the clean towel she knew would be there.

"Cut!" Chris yelled.

She grinned at him before running up the stairs to the guest bathroom.

The shower was hot, but Rochelle's thoughts were hotter. As the water deluged her face, memories of sharing this shower with Grant barraged her senses. Particularly memories of what they did against this wall the last time she was here. The pink ceramic tile, the floral shower curtain, and the little porcelain boy in overalls holding up the toilet paper were not enough to make Rochelle view this room with any sort of innocence ever again. No, these walls had heard too many of her moans of pleasure.

After a few minutes of basking in the steam, the water started to run cold. *Crap*. She forgot that it did that. Now Grant would have to wait another half hour for the water heater to fill up again. She slid the shower curtain away and reached for her towel—only it wasn't there.

Oh my God, I left it in my room.

In fact, she'd left everything in her room. Her clothes, her makeup, her common sense. Yep, it was all sitting there on the bed.

Paralyzed, her mind raced for a solution to this conundrum. Maybe she could wrap toilet paper around the important parts and make a run for it. After all, the bedroom was only a few steps from the bathroom door. The problem was, there was a house full of people right now. What were the chances of not running into anyone?

And more importantly, what were the chances of not running into any cameras? They loved to follow the contestants around the mansion, eavesdropping for gossip and opinions and catfights. More than one shower had been interrupted, and she doubted any of those incidents were accidental. Would they follow her around here? Of course they would.

If Chris shoots me naked, I will shoot him in the head.

She stepped out of the shower and eyed the toilet paper desperately but decided against using it. It would be a pain to peel wet toilet paper off and anyway, wet toilet paper was transparent—and therefore useless.

Then, to her horror, the door opened.

Grant shuffled in, a towel in one arm and clothes in the other. Only after he shut the door did he notice her, standing there in a puddle of water and humiliation. "Rochelle," he said, startled.

His surprise was quickly overtaken by another, more familiar expression. Her first instinct was to cover herself with her hands. But her stronger instinct was to stand there and let him look his fill.

"I seem to have forgotten my towel," she said, feeling heat everywhere. *I'm a fool.*

He stepped forward, meeting her gaze. "I seem to have forgotten my name," he said, licking his lips. "Maybe we could both get in the shower and you could scream it for me."

He took another step forward, his mouth inches from hers. She wouldn't back down. She couldn't. Not when he looked at her that way. Not when she knew he *could* make her scream his name—and she'd enjoy every minute of it. No, she wanted this. And she wanted it badly.

With a new sense of boldness, she leaned into him, her bare breasts brushing against his T-shirt, soaking his chest. Just barely, she glided her lips over his, savoring the taste that was Grant mixed with a hint of blackberry. He allowed her this slow kiss without raising his hands to touch her. It was enough to send shivers throughout her body.

A knock on the door brought them back to reality—and reality TV. Cursing under her breath, Rochelle took a step back, pressing her heels against the tub. She should have taken the opportunity to get her feelings out in the open, not steal a kiss.

Grant sighed, shaking his head. "Yes?" he called.

He handed her his towel, visibly irritated when she

wrapped it around her nakedness.

"Grant?" one of the cameramen—Mike, she thought—said through the door. "Sorry, but Tom and I need a shower before the dinner filming, and we don't have time to go back to the hotel. Your mother sent us up here. How long do you need?"

"I'll be out in ten," Grant said.

"Great. Thanks, man." They heard the shuffle of feet down the hall.

"There's not any hot water left," she stammered. "I…I used it all."

Grant laughed. "Cold water could be very useful right now." She caught his meaning but didn't allow herself to glance below his waist. Mike was coming back in ten minutes. It would only take one of those minutes to get Grant completely out of his clothes.

"I should go," she said, swallowing hard.

He pressed himself against the wall so she could pass. At the door, she turned. "I'll bring you a towel after I'm dressed."

He simply nodded and pulled his shirt off. Leaving wet footprints on Sharon's hardwood hall floor wasn't ideal. But neither was watching Grant undress and not being able to do anything about it. Especially if she was supposed to act natural this evening.

Though kissing Grant did feel like the most natural thing in the world.

Chapter Twenty-Two

He couldn't take his eyes off her sitting across the dinner table, and not just because she'd kissed him earlier. Hell, it wasn't even because she was naked while doing it. After all, it was a small, shy kiss—but it had been a kiss. A real one. And she'd initiated it.

In the space of an evening, Rochelle Ransom had returned to him. Her laugh, her banter, and the alluring way she used to look at him. There was no vile, sacrilegious sweatshirt. There was no clown makeup. There were no whiskey shots.

There was only her.

The problem was, he couldn't figure out why she was acting so…well, *normal*. Was this just a show for his mother? Rochelle had always been fond of his mom, and he wouldn't put it past her to set aside their differences for this segment of the show. Just to spare his mother's feelings.

But she had no idea how much hope she was giving his

mom that they'd reconnected. Sharon would be destroyed if Rochelle rejected him afterward. And so would he.

Of course, he had a little more at stake than his mother did. After all, Mother hadn't been in the bathroom this afternoon when he'd walked in on Rochelle. She could have covered up, she could have screamed, she could have demanded that he leave immediately. But she hadn't. She'd stood there in all her glory and watched him. Dared him with her eyes to touch her.

God, he'd wanted to. But he needed to take it slow. If he had a chance with her at all, things had to be just right. Still, the memory of her made him uncomfortable in his chair. For the fifth time tonight, he was thankful for the tablecloth covering the evidence of his wandering mind. Suddenly, he became aware of a camera pointed directly at him.

"Grant?" his mother said, and by the way she said it, he knew he'd dropped the ball somehow. "Did you hear Rochelle's question?"

"I...I didn't," he sputtered. He looked at Rochelle, apologetic. "Sorry, could you repeat what you said?"

A snort resounded from the camera crew and Grant didn't have to turn his head to know it came from Chris. *Arrogant bastard.*

"Sharon tells me you seldom visit anymore." Rochelle took a sip of her wine. "I was just wondering why."

Of course she would wonder that. This house used to be her home away from home. Her safe haven when her father got abusive or she needed a wholesome meal or she wanted a listening ear. She'd been just as much a fixture here as he was. She would never have understood why he would stay away if he could come here anytime he wanted. She would never have understood that it was all her fault. "I don't know," he said finally. "I guess it's just not the same here without—" *You.* But he couldn't say it. Not yet. Not like this. "Brutus," he finished.

His mother nearly choked on her water. "*Brutus*? You hated that dog!"

He gave her a mild warning look. "Of course I didn't hate him. He was my favorite."

But Rochelle knew how much he'd loathed that ankle-biting Chihuahua. He hoped she could answer the question for herself, while he danced around it for the sake of the camera.

If she did understand, Rochelle didn't let on. She simply proceeded to pepper him with more questions. *Where is your sister? Does she have children? How big was her wedding? What about your brothers? Did they actually mature into men?* He tried to answer her with as much detail as possible without giving away their deception.

When the doorbell rang, a silent awkwardness filled the room. Grant's mother set down her napkin. "I don't know who that could be," she said. "I'm not expecting anyone." But the way the pitch of her voice changed at the end told Grant that she *was* expecting someone—and that someone had just arrived. He had a good idea of who it was—his mother had always been fond of reunions.

Chris looked as though he might swallow his own watch. "Is it imperative that we answer?" he whispered to her pointedly. How many times would Chris butt heads with his mother before he gave up? He knew how stubborn she could be. And Grant knew Chris would never disrespect the woman who practically raised him.

As expected, his mother straightened, lifting her chin. "Of course it is, young man. I'll not stray from my manners just because of your preposterous show."

Rochelle snorted into her napkin, and Grant gave her a wide grin. He'd never heard his mother curse before until earlier today, when she'd referred to Chris as an "uppity ass". Well, maybe he *had* heard her curse before, but not since she'd chased him around their entire property with a switch and an ultimatum.

"Cut," Chris said placidly.

His mother insisted he and Rochelle come to the door to greet the visitor—another sure sign she knew exactly who had dropped by. Both of them were visibly surprised to see Colby Jackson at the threshold. He wore a sport coat and wielded a bouquet of bright blue daisies, which he promptly handed to Grant's mother.

But no one appeared more surprised than Colby. In fact, he could only stare at Rochelle with his mouth gaping open for the next several moments. Chris and the crew had gathered behind them—no telling whether or not they were filming the entrance despite Chris's instructions not to. Colby must have sensed the need for formality because he said, "Rochelle, right?" He extended his hand to her, shaking it gently. "Sharon invited me over to meet you. You must have met with her approval, you see. She won't stop going on about you." So, Colby knew the drill. Then why had he acted so surprised? He looked as though he'd seen an apparition.

Rochelle relaxed instantly, offering a toothy smile. "Colby," she said warmly. "It's...it's so nice to meet you. From what Sharon has said about you, I feel like I've known you all my life."

"Jesus," Chris muttered from behind them. "Let's get on with this. We're rolling in five."

He expressed a desire to only stay for dessert, which Chris reluctantly decided to film for the sake of extra footage, since Colby seemed to be onboard with keeping up the charade. He made it a point to appear fascinated with the process of auditioning as a contestant for the show—something he'd known all about, since he'd been the one to explain it in full detail to Grant.

"So...they pick women who they think will be a good match for the bachelor?" Colby said. "And this is based on some sort of psychological evaluation or something?"

"Yep," Grant replied. "That's how you convinced me to go on the show, remember? All that scientific evidence?" But nothing had convinced him more than Chris telling him that Rochelle was going to be a contestant. Colby had hoped he'd actually find love on this ridiculous show after he voted Rochelle off.

Colby dabbed the corner of his mouth with a napkin. "I didn't realize how accurate they could be."

Rochelle raised a brow. "You and me both."

Grant took a big bite of cobbler while trying to digest what she was saying in code. Did she believe she was the one for him? That they were still compatible? He hoped so.

"So, Rochelle," Colby said. "Why did *you* audition for the show?"

Rochelle didn't miss a beat. "You could say that I haven't been very lucky in love. I was hoping the show would change that."

"Talk about luck with odds," Colby said. His eyes cut to Chris, who scowled at him. "You know, since you're one of the few left and all," he added quickly. "Speaking of odds, you know our Grant here doesn't have such a great track record, either. Has he told you about that?"

Under the table Grant delivered a stout kick to Colby's shin. Colby took it in stride, pretending to have a sudden cough attack. "Excuse me," he said politely. "Cobbler tried to go down the wrong way. You were saying, Rochelle?"

Why is Colby doing this to me?

Rochelle pulled her napkin from her lap and placed it on the table. Grant half expected her to get up and walk away during filming. But she didn't. She picked up her mug and absently stared at the swirling coffee inside. Taking a sip, she finally looked up at Colby again. "He did mention something about it, Colby. He said he broke up with the woman he was going to marry because she was moving on to bigger and better things." Rochelle let her gaze settle on Grant. "You know, Grant, you never told me what those bigger and better things were. I couldn't possibly imagine what would be bigger and better than you."

He sucked in a breath. Was she serious? Or was she just toying with him? First the kiss, now this. "Law school," he said softly. "She was accepted to law school, and I didn't want to hold her back."

"Hmm," she said thoughtfully. "Did she say you were holding her back?"

"No. But I knew I would. She had to move across the country. I knew a long-distance relationship would never work."

"That's interesting. What if she had wanted you to come with her? Would you have gone?"

His heart began to hammer in his chest. She'd really

wanted him to go with her? Could that be true? "I would have absolutely gone with her. All she had to do was ask." But then, he'd never given her the chance, had he? He'd broken up with her, then and there. Yes, it was partly out of anger because she'd gone behind his back and applied for that particular school without his knowledge. Their whole plan had been for her to attend Florida State University so they could be together. He'd never dreamed she meant to take him with her. He'd just assumed she wanted to end it, so he did it first.

"Good to know," she said quietly, taking a sip from her mug.

It was good, good for both of them to know. To get it out in the open, even if it wasn't really the open. He tried to squash the longing rising in him, but he couldn't. Was Rochelle admitting she still wanted him? If so, it was a huge step. One that gave him so much hope, his heart ached.

A sniffle came from the direction of his mother. She had apparently read the same thing into the conversation. He even thought he saw tears welling Rochelle's eyes. He had to change the subject before both of the women in his life sobbed on television for all of America to see.

He looked to Colby, helpless. *Do something*, he said with his eyes. After all, Colby had opened this door. It was his duty to close it again. Luckily, Colby seemed to get the gist. He cleared his throat. "So, Rochelle, Sharon here tells me you're very big into charity work. What cause do you fight for, if I may ask?"

And suddenly Rochelle lit up. Colby didn't talk much the rest of the night—Rochelle hardly let him get a word in after he'd gotten her on the subject of Helping Hands. Grant enjoyed hearing her speak about something so passionately. He'd missed her passion and her love for helping others. He'd missed everything about her.

After Colby's departure, Grant's mother revealed that she made not one blackberry cobbler, but two, and she invited the crew to sit and have some. Delighted, they bashfully took their seats at the table—even Chris, who had seemed self-absorbed since returning from the interview.

Grant's mom set clean plates on the table and gathered up the dirty ones. "Won't you help your mother with the dishes?"

"Of course," he said at the same time Rochelle said, "I'll help."

His mother waved a hand at her. "You go sit on the front porch swing, darling. After the crew has their dessert, they can film you and Grant having some one-on-one time."

Even Chris seemed pleased at this prospect. But with Sharon Drake, Grant knew nothing was ever so simple. When they reached the kitchen, she whirled on him. "Go retrieve Rochelle from the porch. Here are the keys to the truck."

What? "What?"

She huffed in frustration. "I've got the crew distracted. Now you two can escape and actually talk for once."

His mother was brilliant. "Where will we go?"

She gave him a thoughtful look. "I'd offer to take her by her old house."

"She hated that place, Mom."

"Time puts everything into perspective, son. Besides, it's just a house. She's already *home* here."

A pang of anguish lodged in Grant's chest. "Mom, you

shouldn't get your hopes up—"

"I'm quite certain I didn't raise an idiot, boy, so I'm not sure why you're still standing there."

Rochelle sucked in a breath as they pulled into the driveway of her childhood home. The drive had been silent, full of mutual contemplation. Grant wasn't sure where to start. He didn't want to blurt out his feelings, but he was on the verge of doing just that. If she rejected him though, it would pulverize his heart.

"It looks exactly the same," she said as he put the truck in park. "Except—where are all the trees? Where is my treehouse?" She had never referred to it as *her* treehouse before. She had always felt that since the people who lived there before had built it for their daughter, it still belonged to her in some way. Especially after she'd fallen out of it years ago. She'd taken it as a sign to stay away from it.

Grant gave her a sidelong look. "Mom says a bad storm took all the trees out. The whole neighborhood helped to clear them. Treehouse and all."

"Hmmm."

"We don't have to get out," he said. "If you don't want to."

She opened the door. "What would be the point in that? We came all this way. And the moon is bright. We'll be able to see all the way around the house. *All* my memories here weren't bad, you know." With a mischievous grin, she shut the door and walked up the concrete path to the worn-down house.

His pulse picked up a beat as he realized to which memories she was referring. The couch. Her bed. Even the kitchen table hadn't been safe from them in those rare times they'd found themselves alone here.

Rochelle tried the door but found it locked. She peered in through the living room window. "Wow, it's so...small."

"Or it could be that you feel equal to it now," he said quietly. "Small" was one word she had used to describe herself when she was younger. Small compared to the house, the world. Her father. But she was successful now. She'd made something of herself. And she'd left this place behind in her dust.

She nodded without looking at him. "I think you're right. Even turning down this road used to leave my stomach a mess. Now there's... nothing." She turned to him. "I didn't think such a strong hatred could ever go away."

"Hatred is a poisonous emotion to hold onto," he said. "Especially if it stops you from being happy."

They seemed to realize at the same time that his words carried a different meaning. For so many years, she'd harbored a hatred for something other than this house. And though she'd been entitled to it, he fervently hoped she'd let that go.

"I've been thinking about that actually. Grant—"

"Rochelle," he said, taking a step toward her. When she didn't stop him, he pulled her into his arms. She readily accepted him and wrapped her arms around his waist. "Rochelle, am I dreaming this? Are you really here with me again?" A tear slipped down her cheek, and he caught it at her chin with the crook of his finger. "I've never stopped loving you, Chelle. I've never stopped thinking about you. I was angry that you would leave me. I never dreamed you would want me to come. If I'd known, I would have up and left in a heartbeat, no questions asked. Please forgive me. I need you to forgive me. I need *you*."

He lowered his mouth but only brushed her lips. He wanted her, all of her, but she had to give him permission before he could allow himself access to her again.

She opened her mouth to him, letting her tongue drizzle his bottom lip, teasing and testing and driving him mad. She was still shy at his touch, still holding back from letting go completely. He didn't have the patience for patience, he decided. He had to show her what they still were. What they still had. But not here. Not now. He wanted—needed—to take his time with her. To bring her to the full realization that she didn't belong anywhere but with him.

His hands slid down her waist to the back of her skirt where he cupped both cheeks and gripped her tightly to him, pressing her into his hardness. She moaned against him as he demanded she open wider. Hungrily, she complied.

Their tongues, their arms, their bodies tangled together. There wasn't an inch of her that he didn't cover, not a curve that he didn't explore with his hands. It felt new yet familiar, and satisfying and yet not enough. It would never be enough, not with Rochelle. He wanted her, all of her, and all the time. It was an exquisite torture that he allowed himself, even though he knew he had to end it soon, before he led her to the truck and took her then and there. His mother's truck would simply not do for this reunion.

It was almost painful to pull away, but it had to be done, even as she grasped him tighter. If he didn't stop this now, he would have taken her on the nearest available horizontal surface. While she seemed willing at the moment, she'd have plenty of time to think about what they'd done on the plane back to the mansion, and he didn't want her to have a single regret. Slowly, against his will, he pried her from his grip.

She pouted up at him. "You're kidding, right?" she said, breathless.

He laughed, kissing her again. "I was thinking of a… more appropriate setting."

"Hmm. We've never cared about the setting before."

"It's just that I can't shake the memory of you stepping out of the shower this afternoon." He ran his lips along her neck, nibbling here and there and reveling in the fact that she shivered in the heat of a Southern July. "Will you indulge me?"

"The camera crew will be waiting for something like that!" she hissed, as if they were already hovering somewhere in the bushes.

"We'll throw them off. Pretend to be fighting when we get back. They'll probably call it a night and go back to the hotel. They've fallen into a routine with us, don't you think?"

"Your mother will be home."

"Then try not to scream too loudly."

Chapter Twenty-Three

Breakfast with the Drakes was nothing less than painful. Sharon prattled on about mundane things like needing to change the seed in her birdfeeders that afternoon, but Rochelle was pretty sure she knew what had happened last night. In fact, she was pretty sure the next-door neighbors could give a play-by-play of last night's excitement. And this morning's. And all the time in between.

Grant moved food around his plate without looking up or even attempting conversation. He looked tired, and he very well should have been. They'd reinvented the all-nighter, after all. And boy, Christopher Schnartz-Legend was not happy about the new developments—even though he didn't know exactly what those developments were. All he knew for sure was that they'd taken a drive out to her childhood home. And he hadn't been happy about it. Especially since he could tell, seething from his seat in the corner nook, that the universe had shifted last night. Anyone could tell.

Rochelle tried to appreciate the quiche Sharon had made, but her thoughts kept straying to her futile attempt at showering this morning. How Grant had lifted her against the wall and made good on his promise to make her scream. Thank goodness Sharon's bedroom was on the first floor. But more likely than not, she'd already been awake and in the kitchen preparing breakfast for everyone. Rochelle cringed inwardly.

"Mrs. Drake," Chris said, wrapping his hands around his mug as if to keep them warm. "I think it would be best if a small crew slept here for the rest of the home visit. It's just for one night. Could you accommodate that?"

Sharon scowled, glancing at Grant. "I have another spare room but it'll only sleep two people who are willing to share the same bed."

"Sounds like someone's sleeping on the floor then," Chris drawled.

"Or you could just let these two be for the rest of the visit and give them some privacy."

"Privacy makes for poor ratings, Mrs. Drake. Besides, these two already forfeited their right to privacy when they auditioned for the show." He cut his eyes to Rochelle and Grant. "So their leaving last night without the crew could be considered a breech in—"

"Alright, alright," Grant said waving his hand. "We get it. We stay with the crew. It won't happen again."

Rochelle swallowed disappointment along with her orange juice. They'd have to stay away from each other for a while to throw off any suspicion that they were back together. They had discussed how this would work, and Grant had already anticipated Chris throwing a tantrum about their field trip last night. They'd decided to keep outward appearances as they had been; Rochelle would continue her stunts and Grant would continue to be a good sport about it. Having them appear as rivals would be the only way they might be able to steal private moments when they were back on the set of *Luring Love*.

It seemed silly to stay on the show, because they knew what the outcome would be. It felt like a waste of time to put off starting their new life together when they had so much making up to do as it was. But they were both under obligation to see it through, and besides, they both agreed that Helping Hands needed the double prize money. What was a few more weeks in the grand scheme of the rest of their lives?

Still, it would be difficult to stay away from Grant now that she'd had him at her fingertips all night. There was so much more of him she wanted to explore—and not just underneath his clothes. She'd missed out on a decade of Grant and she was determined to get it back, one way or the other.

If behaving herself now would gain her the ability to sneak around the set for the duration of the show, then she could show some patience.

At least, she hoped she could.

Chapter Twenty-Four

Grant shut the door to Richie's office and took a seat in front of his desk. It had been nice to get away from the producer's prying eyes for a while. But he never completely escaped while he'd been away on home visits. Chris had seen to that. His childhood friend took his job very seriously. But he couldn't be too upset about it. After all, Chris was partly responsible for his winning Rochelle back. If it weren't for him, Grant would have never been considered for the show, and Rochelle might have actually pursued another man.

Just the thought made him clench his jaw.

"You wanted to see me?" Grant said, gruffer than he'd intended.

Richie didn't pretend to hide his irritation. "Chris tells me you and Rochelle went off together. Alone. Do explain."

He had to handle this delicately; Richie was no fool. It was Rochelle who'd suggested they play the game until the end. And when she'd explained why, he'd agreed wholeheartedly. Now he had to convince Richie that there was nothing between them—and that there never would be. "It had to happen eventually, and we couldn't very well do it on camera," Grant said, trying to sound defeated.

"Please tell me you're not referring to sleeping with each other, because that very well *could* have been done on—"

Grant balled his fists until his knuckles strained against his skin. He imagined tightening Richie's necktie until he turned as purple as the tacky violet suit he wore. "We had the talk," Grant said instead.

This seemed to startle the producer. "*The* talk? And what did she say?"

"That's not your business."

Richie pouted. "Now that hurts, Grant. You know I've grown fond of you two. It's only natural that I ask. I wonder if Rochelle would tell me?"

They'd foreseen this. And Rochelle had already practiced what she would say if Richie asked her the same questions. Grant shrugged. "Doubtful. She's not an idiot. We both know you only care to know whether or not she's staying on the show."

The older man stiffened. "It's a valid question at this point, I think. And regardless of how you two feel about each other, I do have a job to do. Our high ratings this season have a lot to do with the chemistry between you two. I do hope that's not going to change."

"She's staying." Grant sighed. "Though she doesn't want to. We talked about it briefly at the airport. There's a lot more that needs to be worked out between us than can be accomplished on this show. Just so you know, she told me about Helping Hands. I won't vote her off, so you can stop asking me about it." Giving Richie some inside information would throw him off their trail for a while.

As planned, Richie seemed pleased to be let in on a secret. "Well. I knew you were a gentleman, Grant. And of course, it's excellent news that she's staying, one way or the other. I do hope you won't give up in winning her over though."

"I'm a fool to keep trying." They still had to make it look like they were at odds. The only way Grant could envision that happening was to play the pathetic, lovesick sucker. It was an easy part to perform; all he had to do was imagine that Rochelle had rejected him at her parents' old house. Then he really would be a groveling idiot right now.

"Gentlemen usually are." Richie leaned forward. "So, she's not ready to forgive you yet?"

He shook his head. "But it's my fault, so what can I really say?"

Richie smiled, more to himself than at Grant. It was the kind of smile a canary-swallowing cat would give his oblivious owner. What was Richie up to? "Chris tells me you had a visitor at your mother's house. Colby, was it? Why on earth would a mother name her son after cheese?"

"What do you care about Colby?"

Richie shrugged. "Chris said he brought up some points that he was sure would sway Rochelle in your favor. I suppose Chris was wrong."

"He was wrong. I saw him talking to Colby privately. I hope he didn't say anything too incriminating about me." Because if Colby had snitched on their business phone calls, he'd make sure his friend never lived it down. He was fairly certain Colby and Chris had just been catching up on old times. And probably gossiping like old women about what had been going on between himself and Rochelle.

Richie gave him an amused look. This made Grant nervous. Maybe Colby had snitched after all. Was Richie about to ask him to forfeit his cell phone? That would throw a wrench in his plans with Rochelle; before they left his home, he'd smuggled her his mother's cell phone to use.

Richie leaned back in his chair, the leather squeaking beneath his weight. "Well," Richie said, suddenly appearing bored. "All the girls are settled back into the mansion and everything is all set for the Double Elimination Ceremony. You have major interviews for the next two weeks that you'd do well not to screw up, so go get some rest. You're already a celebrity—this could be good opportunity for your business." He paused, pressing his fingertips together. "You probably already know who you're going to vote off." But he held up his hand abruptly. "Do *not* tell me, Grant Drake. Even I like surprises."

"Since when?"

"Run along now. You're distracting me."

Chris was waiting for Grant outside Richie's office. No cameras, no crew. Just Chris. "Did you sort everything out with Rochelle the other night?" he asked.

Grant wanted to brush him off. But Chris's concern seemed genuine. He felt guilty about it, but he had to throw his friend off their scent too. Chris was entirely too committed to his new job to trust him with any information about him and Rochelle. "Yes. If by sorting everything out, you mean making an idiot out of myself and hurting her more."

Chris grimaced. "I knew where you had gone, you know. It wasn't too difficult to figure out, though your mother would rather have bitten off her own tongue than tell me. If she ever needs a job with the FBI, I know a guy. That nut cannot be cracked."

Grant chuckled. "So why didn't you come after us?"

Chris scratched the back of his neck. "Because not everything belongs on camera. Even I know that."

"Do you?"

His friend sighed. "I know I've been a dick lately and I'm sorry. But this job is important to me, man. It's a stepping stone to bigger and better things. If I don't please Richie, then I don't please the network. If I don't please the network, my career in television is practically over."

"What are you saying?"

"I'm saying that whatever happens, I don't want it to affect our friendship."

"You've got a job to do, and I get that." It was all Grant could afford to say. Chris had all but said he would do what it took to keep his boss happy. That meant he couldn't be trusted until after the publicity from the show died down. It meant that he and Rochelle could expect zero privacy from then on. It was a friendly warning, and Grant appreciated it.

"Goodnight, Chris."

"Goodnight."

It had been a long time since Grant had snuck into a woman's bedroom—ten years, in fact. Rochelle's dorm room had been on the first floor though—nothing like climbing to the second floor of the bachelorette mansion. Grant was a bit disappointed with the security of the place, truth be told. No one should have been able to successfully scale the wall and land on the balcony of her room without being detected—not even him. The mansion needed about a dozen upgrades on their security system, at the very least.

Not that he could mention that to Richie without sounding suspicious.

Grant nearly tripped over a dying potted plant as he made his way in the dark to the door of the balcony, where light splayed from sheer curtains. He peered in, spotting Maya and Rochelle sitting on their beds. Tapping lightly on the glass, he alerted them to his presence.

Maya rose and let him in. "You're early," she whispered unnecessarily. The pathetic security guard probably didn't even patrol this side of the mansion. Grant hadn't seen him in at least half an hour.

"Sorry. I didn't anticipate being able to get in so easily."

She rolled her eyes. "Show off."

Grant chuckled as he crossed the threshold into the bedroom. Maya had been an invaluable resource these past two weeks. Whenever he could steal some time with Rochelle between interviews and promotions, Maya made it her job to distract the camera crew. She'd become quite the drama queen, to Richie's delight. She'd started a small fire in the kitchen last week by microwaving tin foil, and two days ago, she'd started a catfight with Cassandra over the use of a treadmill in the mansion's gym. She still had a scratch running down the length of her cheek to show for it. She'd called it a worthy war wound.

Rochelle smiled up at Maya. "How much time do you think we'll have tonight?"

Maya shrugged. "A good two hours, I think. I'm planning

to fake a drowning in the pool. Leg cramp."

"Brilliant," Rochelle said.

Maya made her way to the door. "Don't make any noise this time, okay? Jacquelyn already told Chris she thought the place was haunted. All the moaning and such coming from our floor."

Rochelle blushed, which he found exceedingly amusing. "We'll only be talking tonight."

"We will?" Grant said, doubtful. He'd already sized up her rather modest pajamas and decided they had to go. Of course, he always thought her clothes would look better on the floor.

She raised her chin, determined. "Yes. Talking." She pointed to Maya's bed across from her. "You're staying there, and I'm staying here."

Two hours of talking? It would never happen. At least, it hadn't happened recently, anyway. Keeping their hands off each other just wasn't their specialty. But to appease Rochelle, Grant sat on Maya's bed and leaned on his elbow. "All set then."

After Maya left to wreak havoc, Rochelle rested on her elbow on her own bed. "We're going to play twenty questions for real this time. And no stupid questions, like favorite color or anything."

They'd had little time to talk since leaving his mother's house. Or rather, they'd *made* little time for talk, using their privacy for more strenuous physical activities. When they'd had the chance to chat here and there, they'd always talked about their future together. Playing twenty questions gave them a chance to talk about their past. "Okay. Got it. You first." He brought his legs up on the bed and relaxed. If

Rochelle was serious about talking, he would make it work. For tonight.

"Was there anyone after me? I mean, was there anyone that you…cared for?"

It was an easy question. "Never. Dates and one-night stands. Never anything serious. You?"

She bit her lip. "Same here. Your turn."

"Okay. Let's see…" The question he really wanted to ask was at the tip of his tongue, but it had the potential to ruin the evening. The last thing he wanted to do was fight with Rochelle Ransom ever again. But he had to know. "Why didn't you check in with my mom after you left?" His mother had been hurt by their breakup, but not hearing from Rochelle ever again had hurt her more. Of course, he'd wanted to let things like that go. But he had to know why she never called.

This caught her by surprise, he could tell. She took one of the fluffy throw pillows on her bed and tucked it to her chest. "Because she reminded me so much of you. Her laugh, the way she says thing, the way she winks at me. I couldn't see her, because I wasn't ready to see you. I never meant to hurt her."

Fair enough. He wondered how he would have felt if he'd seen Rochelle's mother again. He supposed the phone calls and checking in worked both ways. After Rochelle left, he never bothered to pick up the phone, either. "Your turn to ask, I think."

"Okay, what was your least favorite moment on this show so far?"

"That's easy. It was when one of the evil contestants drop-kicked my balls."

She giggled. "I was mad, because I thought you were going to use the opportunity to fondle all the contestants. It's not like they were really going to try to defend themselves against your wandering hands."

He raised a brow. "Rochelle, why do you think I teach women self-defense classes? You've got to know, it has everything to do with you, with how you grew up."

She bit her lip. "It was something I refused to acknowledge at the time."

"And now?"

"And now I know you really do care. That you were affected by what happened all those years ago."

Judging from the tears welling in her eyes, he decided a change of subject was in order. Watching Rochelle Ransom suffer at the hands of her past wasn't something he wanted to see tonight. "What about you? Your least favorite moment?"

"God, I have to pick just one? Well, there was the puking on the plane incident. Not my proudest moment. I can't believe you made me go first!"

Grant chuckled. "You asked for it! The garden maze stunt was demoralizing."

She snickered. "That was actually fun. And I needed that nap, too. Let me see…Oh." She wrinkled her nose at him. "I hated the part where you had to take each contestant to the Paradise Suite. I wouldn't let myself admit it, but I couldn't bear the idea you might sleep with any of them."

"Nothing happened, you know."

"Yes, I know," she smiled. "All those walnut cookies probably had you covered in welts in places even I've never seen."

"Ha! Maya told you, huh? What was I supposed to do,

anyway? Sleep with all those women while I was trying to win you back?"

"You didn't want to sleep with any of them?"

"When I had the chance of having *you*? Absolutely not."

She took a moment to process that. "When did you decide you wanted me back?"

He wiped his hand down his face, frustrated by the memory of it. "Well, first of all, I never wanted to let you go in the first place. But if you're talking about on the show, then it was that damn kissing booth. It drove me insane. And then our kiss was…a powerful reminder of how much I missed you."

"What about Tiffany Wallace?" she blurted.

"Tiffany Wallace was—and is—nothing to me. I'm sorry that I hurt you over someone so insignificant. I wish I could take it back."

"I wish I could un-see you kissing her."

Just then, they heard the far off cry of an ambulance. They exchanged looks. "You don't think that's for Maya—" Rochelle said.

"We'd better go check it out." If Maya actually *had* drowned…

"We can't get caught together," she protested. "I'll leave the room first. You wait a few minutes before you come downstairs."

"Chelle, I'm not even supposed to be here. But I suppose I could use this as an opportunity to show Richie just how sorry the security is around here."

She rolled her eyes. "Let's go." She made her way out the door and down the hall. When he could hear her tennis shoes on the stairwell, he followed behind at a slower pace. At the bottom of the stairwell Rochelle rounded the corner—and stopped abruptly. "Richie!" she said loudly. "You startled me."

"Did I?" Grant heard him say, sounding undeterred. "I'm so sorry to tell you this, dear, but we've called an ambulance for Maya. It seems that woman has gotten herself into another mishap, and she's just about drowned. Did she mention anything to you about going to the pool?"

Rochelle nodded to Richie, who Grant still couldn't see behind the wall. "Yes, she said it had been a long time since she'd taken a swim."

"Hmm. Interesting. When she filled out her questionnaire for the show, she indicated that she didn't know how to swim. Funny that she would get in a pool with no lifeguard, not knowing how to swim, don't you think?" He stepped forward, into Grant's line of view. Grant slid behind the wall at the head of the stairs. "You know what else is interesting, Ms. Ransom? The fact that Maya has been acting so...well, so much like *you* lately. At first I was delighted, of course, because scandal is a ratings booster. But after a while, I thought that these little displays just didn't make much sense. Maya is very down to earth and has been since the start of the show. Much like you would be, if you didn't have your own agenda, right?" Grant didn't like this line of questioning. Richie was too curious, and too observant. They'd have to be a lot more careful from now on.

"Well, maybe she does have an agenda," Rochelle said. "It is a game, after all. Maybe she's finally started to play it. You'd have to talk to her about that, though."

"Perhaps I will."

"I was just checking to see what the sirens were all

about. I hope Maya is going to be okay," Rochelle said.

"Oh, I think she'll be just fine. It was nice chatting with you, Ms. Ransom."

"See you later, Richie."

Grant could hear Rochelle bound up the stairs. She didn't look at him when she passed him on the top, just kept walking toward the room she shared with Maya. Richie must have still been watching her. At the door, she paused and gave him a warning look. "He's still down there," she mouthed.

Rochelle's eyes got wide when they heard a second set of steps making their way up the stairwell. Grant decided it was time to go. Richie was apparently already suspicious that something was going on under his nose, and Grant wasn't about to give him more fuel for that fire. He backed up quietly to the next room, and finding it empty, shut the door swiftly behind him. Luckily, the room had a window. Add that to the piss poor security of the mansion in general and Grant could make a clean getaway easily. Richie would be none the wiser.

He landed effortlessly on the sidewalk running between the east and west wings on the mansion. As he dodged each surveillance camera on the way back to his room, he contemplated the package he'd received from Colby this morning. It had been filled with documents he needed to sign in order to keep their business running smoothly. But taped to one of the papers in the middle of the stack had been a diamond ring. A ring he'd been too stubborn to retrieve from his pocket ten years ago.

If he could, Grant would walk onto the veranda, grab the two bouquets of sweet peas, throw them at Cassandra and Jacquelyn, and flip off the camera as he stalked away. Tonight would be the Double Elimination round, and he couldn't be happier about it. Tonight he would narrow down the competition to two finalists, Rochelle and Maya. Or at least, that's what Richie and Chris thought.

Absently, he reached into his pocket and clutched the ring there. He'd decided he was sick of this game and sick of being apart from Rochelle even a second longer. Tonight he hoped to change everything. Tonight he hoped to correct the wrongs of the past.

Chris interrupted his line of thought. "Richie wants you to drag this episode out. We've got a lot of sponsors to please, so the more painstaking the decision, the better."

"Richie is sick."

Chris gave him a crooked smile. "He's a bastard, yes. But his instincts with ratings are uncanny."

Grant followed Chris to the pedestal where two bouquets of sweet peas resided. "Why did you choose to be a reality show host anyway?" Grant grumbled. "You could have been an actor, maybe in one of those comic book movies. You'd look cute in tights." In a way he felt guilty about what he was about to do. Still, both Chris and Richie would get their precious ratings, he was sure of it.

Chris smirked. "You always did like my ass."

"No, I always *kicked* your ass. There's a difference."

Chris held up his hands in surrender. "Touché. Look, ratings seem like a shallow concern now. But wait until the Golden Rose Ceremony. Then maybe you'll appreciate Richie's drive for audience captivation."

"What do you mean?"

"All I can say is that the finale will go out with a bang. Now wait here. It's time to start." Chris turned to the camera. "We're rolling in two! Everyone take your places!"

Within minutes Chris was inviting the last four contestants out onto the veranda. Maya, Rochelle, Cassandra, and Jacquelyn made their way through the French doors. Chris ushered them in to sit on the edge of the fountain. "Tonight will be a sad farewell to two of you lovely ladies. Before we speak to Grant about the choices he's made though, we want to take a minute to review the time each of you have spent on the show so far."

Grant cracked his knuckles nervously as two men in tuxedos wheeled out a flatscreen TV sitting on a cheesy golden cart sprinkled with pink rose petals. For the next ten minutes, the contestants would watch footage of themselves and supposedly think about what they could have done differently to increase their chances of staying on the show. For the next ten minutes, he would have to relive the humiliation this show has caused him.

Sheer ridiculousness.

The video began with Maya's expression when she saw Grant for the first time. Her smile was radiant, breathtaking. In the background, the sound of shattering glass could be heard. The screen switched to the fundraiser, showing Maya working in her booth and greeting Grant with a shy grin. Next up was their dinner; their one-on-one date; meeting her father at the airport; lying in the back of a truck bed with Grant. Last, the clip showed some behind-the-scenes footage. Maya getting ready in Wardrobe and Makeup, Maya ripping her tight dress and uttering an expletive that only she could make sound lady-like, Maya jumping out of the closet and scaring one of the twins. By the end of the clip, Maya was in tears.

"That was beautiful, Chris," she sniffled. "Thank you." Maya was a good friend and a good faker.

Chris's smile was kind. "You've been a wonderful addition to the show, Maya. Good luck to you." He settled his gaze on Rochelle. "Next, we'll get to see Rochelle in action."

Rochelle was shown dropping her wine glass—an image Grant would never forget; Rochelle staggering through the garden maze in a drunken stupor; Rochelle kissing a handsome patron at her kissing booth; her attempt to puke outside of the plane, and failing miserably at it; her comforting Ellie at the dinner table; her getting her lips stained with a certain blackberry cobbler. The behind-the-scenes footage revealed Rochelle looking longingly at Grant as he talked to Chris before a show; her glaring at some of the other contestants while they chattered in the mansion's living room about Grant's exceptional body; the silhouette of Rochelle and Grant's mother walking down the lane illuminated by white Christmas lights.

Grant didn't even know that had happened.

To a stranger, Rochelle might have appeared unaffected by the video. But by the way she shifted from one foot to the other, Grant knew that she was very moved. It had been a long show for both of them. But at least it had been worth it. And it was almost over.

Absently, he watched the other two videos for Cassandra and Jacquelyn. He vaguely remembered the list of "don'ts" he'd received from Jacquelyn's father. For Cassandra's turn, they chose to show the food-fight fiasco and Cassandra's mother slapping him upon entering their house for the first time.

And just as he thought the clip would come to an end, the screen revealed the kiss he and Cassandra had shared in the Dream Suite. Cassandra, in her nearly naked glory, pressed against him, her mouth on his, and her hands everywhere they could reach.

Grant immediately cut his eyes to Rochelle and cringed. She stood there watching in apt attention, a scowl etched onto her face. *Not good.*

As the video came to an end, Grant hurriedly picked up the first bouquet of sweet peas from the pedestal, not waiting for Chris's cue. Then he picked up the other. Chris gave him a look of warning. Oh, right. He was supposed to make this painstakingly slow. He set one bouquet back in place and tucked the other under his arm without thinking.

Grant walked down the line of contestants, who were all in different states of nervousness—save Rochelle, who wouldn't so much as look at him—as they watched him pace in front of where they sat on the edge of the fountain. The entire set was so quiet that the only sounds were Grant's footsteps and the gentle lull of cascading water. Finally, he turned to face the ladies. He still wasn't sure where to begin. He knew who was leaving, but he didn't want to drag it out for ten years like Richie wanted him to. He wanted it done and over with, so the finale could be done and over with and his new life with Rochelle would start.

The only thing he was sure of was *who* to begin with.

"Rochelle," he said. "Please stand."

She complied, her eyes glistening with emotion. He remembered her saying she wished she could un-see his kiss with Tiffany Wallace. Now he wished she could un-see the kiss he shared with Cassandra.

"I was extremely touched by your video," he told her. "While watching it, I began to realize that your feelings for me may be deeper than what we both might have imagined. Which is something that makes me extremely happy. Honestly, I've grown very attached to you over the course of the show. In the beginning, you didn't seem to adjust well. You didn't try to make friends with the contestants. You didn't try to make friends with me. It almost felt as if you truly didn't want to be here." He took her hands in his. "I hope that's no longer the case."

When she didn't respond, Grant sucked in a galvanizing breath. How long did he have to babble on? "I think that night with Ellie was a turning point for me," he continued for the sake of the show. "You handled the situation with such compassion and kindness. I knew then that you were one to watch in the competition. And so I have." He caressed her cheek with his thumb and she gave him a look filled with questions and most importantly, a look meant to show that she was outwardly torn. God, but she was a good actress. He almost believed that she wanted to tuck her tail and run off the set. He wondered what the audience would see when they viewed her expression from the comfort of their homes, without knowing what had happened between them. Would they buy it? "What you've shown me since then, I've liked a lot. And for that reason, I'm keeping you on the show. Please do me the honor of staying for the Golden Rose Ceremony?"

Her eyes grew round as half dollars. Still, she said nothing, offering a slight nod and seating herself back on the edge of the fountain. Her posture was stiff; she carefully trained her eyes on the cobblestones of the veranda. Grant would pay a billion pennies for a glimpse into her thoughts at this moment. She was supposed to be acting resistant—and she was doing a bang up job at it. She almost had him convinced she didn't want to be there.

And so with as much patience as he could muster, he dawdled before presenting Cassandra and Jacquelyn with the bouquets of sweet peas. He gave Jacquelyn her arrangement first, letting her down gently. But when he got to Cassandra, she snatched the bouquet from his hands, threw the flowers to the ground, and stomped on them as best she could in heels.

"You, sir, are not a gentleman," she bellowed. "You used me for sex! And now this is how you're going to treat me?"

Grant felt a cold shiver of dread steal through him. Chris was at his side instantly. "Cassandra, what do you mean Grant used you for sex?"

"I mean that Grant and I have been sleeping together for the entire show. He told me I was the one! He said he didn't care about anyone else here. He even told me to keep the walnut allergy a secret. That he only used that excuse so he didn't have to sleep with the other contestants."

The walnut allergy? As far as he knew, Maya had been the only one to figure it out. And he knew Rochelle wouldn't have said anything about it. What the hell was going on? Deep down though, he knew.

Chris peered up at Grant, eyes wide. "Grant? What do you have to say about these accusations?"

But Grant was too furious to answer. This was obviously all Richie's doing—and Chris had helped him. Hell, he'd practically apologized in advance for his betrayal tonight. Grant and Rochelle had stolen time to themselves, now Richie was making them pay for it and Chris was acting like his little puppet.

Grant turned to Rochelle. She was completely buying into Cassandra's performance, which infuriated him even further. Tears spilled down her cheeks, and her lips turned down in a scowl. Even Maya pulled her friend close, whispering consoling words in her ear. Did Maya believe Cassandra, too? Surely they could see that he clearly wasn't kissing Cassandra back in the Dream Suite. Couldn't they?

"He told me he loved me," Cassandra sobbed on. "And he told me that I would win the show. That it was a done deal. He said he was tired of trying to get back the love of his life. That he wanted me to be the one."

I haven't even said a word, Grant thought, *and Rochelle believes everything coming out of Cassandra's mouth.*

So, he hadn't won Rochelle back, not completely. Part of her still hadn't forgiven the past, a part that couldn't quite overcome the hurt he'd caused her. He'd specifically told her he hadn't slept with anyone on the show. That there had only been her. He'd spent every last available moment with her since they'd returned from the home visit. How could she be falling for this ruse that Richie—and obviously Chris—had cooked up?

But by the way Rochelle looked at him now, he would never have all of her no matter what he did. They had taken some big steps in the past two weeks. Maybe they should have slowed down and really taken their time to get to know each other again. By the way he'd acted, she probably did think him a sex-crazed fool. First she'd seen him with

Tiffany Wallace all those years ago and now she saw him with Cassandra.

Maybe he should have given Rochelle more time to trust him again, more time for her to know that he only ever wanted what was best for her. More talking, less sex. But it was too late, he could see that.

There would never be enough trust between them now. Richie had put Cassandra up to this. Or maybe Cassandra had done it herself just to get some last-minute attention. But Richie would never come clean and admit his involvement, and Cassandra would never admit her lies. Chris wouldn't be of any help, either; he had already stooped to a level lower than Grant ever imagined he would to keep his new career. Still, Grant could tell Rochelle all of that, and she wouldn't believe him, at least fully. It was all over her face.

Slowly, he removed the mic from his suit jacket and handed it to Chris. "I'm done."

And then he walked off the veranda.

Chapter Twenty-Five

Maya burst through their bedroom door, breathless. Rochelle tried her best to ignore her and proceeded to load folded clothes into her suitcase. She'd thought she'd have time to get it done before her roommate came back from the gym. All she had to do now was tell Richie she was through.

"What are you doing?" Maya asked. "Why are you packing?"

"Isn't it obvious? I'm leaving," she replied in a clipped tone. "I can't stand to be here another second. I can't stand to be around *him* another second."

"You're not leaving," Maya said, closing the distance between them. She grabbed Rochelle's shoulders and gave her good shake. "You'll lose the money for Helping Hands if you quit."

Rochelle eased out of her grip and sat on the bed next to her stack of clothes. Damn the tears that threatened to spill over. "Sometimes money isn't everything." Not when her heart was breaking like this, all over again. It felt doubly worse than last time, because this time, Grant's crime was much more serious. Last time he'd broken up with her so she'd be free to go to college. He'd said Tiffany had meant nothing to him, but how would she ever know for sure? Maybe he'd been with Tiffany the entire time he was dating her. And now, this.

This time, he'd lied to her face and slept with someone else while trying to convince her he wanted her and her alone. Cassandra had even known about his walnut allergy, and how he'd used it to ward off the sexual advances of the other contestants. Cassandra had been the one to cry foul, but the truth was, he'd used them both. How long had he been like that? And how could she ever face him again?

Maya sat across from her. "Listen, maybe you should hear him out."

"I'm not answering his phone calls. He had a chance to deny it on national television and didn't—or couldn't. Now he's had enough time to come up with a lie to smooth things over. It's not happening. I'm done."

"It's just that he seemed so sincere. He's crazy about you. I know it. Maybe he just—"

"It doesn't matter why he did it. He lied to me. I can't trust him." And the idea of him sleeping with Cassandra the entire time made her nauseous. She'd winced when he'd admitted there had been one-night stands since he'd been with her, but it was nothing compared to knowing the woman in the flesh and imagining her naked with the man she loved. Imagining her being intimate with him in the same way she had been with him these past two weeks. Had he done the same things with her as he'd done with Cassandra?

She closed her eyes against the images conjured up by that question.

That Grant hadn't said anything at all to defend himself during the show told her everything she needed to know. She wouldn't buy into his lies ever again.

"Rochelle, think of all that money you're losing for Helping Hands," Maya pleaded. "There's one more elimination ceremony. Let's give him a taste of his own medicine. If he picks you, humiliate him. If he picks me, I'll humiliate him. But don't walk away on that money. You've stayed so long already and endured so much."

"I don't know if I can face him again," she said, catching the tears on her chin with the back of her hand.

"You can do this. I'll be there with you. Remember, you didn't come on this show for you. You came on this show for something bigger than you. Don't lose sight of that."

Rochelle sat on the bed and sniffled. "You're right. It's just one more show. I don't have to talk to him. I don't even have to look at him if I don't want to." In fact, she just had to show up to the ceremony. If that was all that was keeping her from the prize money, she'd be a fool not to man up and go through with it. "All right. I'll stay."

The morning of the Golden Rose Ceremony, Richie called Rochelle into his office. "I've wired the money into your account as agreed," he said before she was even seated.

"That's awfully bold of you. What if I don't show up

tonight?" Because at that moment, she felt like bolting. What was keeping her here now? Nothing, not even Maya's pep talk.

Richie leaned back in his chair and pressed his fingertips together. "The Double Elimination Ceremony was a shock to us all. I mean, who would have thought he'd been sneaking around with Cassandra?"

A shock? What a gross understatement. It had been devastating. And she certainly didn't want to rehash that night with Richie. Not when her stomach twisted each time she thought of Grant and Cassandra together. "What can I do for you, Richie?"

"I'm willing to let you out of our verbal agreement. You can fly out this morning; in fact, I already have a plane booked for you."

She leaned back in her chair. "And why would you do that?" Richie was not the generous type; there had to be a catch.

"Because even I have a heart, Ms. Ransom. Besides, you're not bringing anything to the show anymore. Your stunts have become subpar and unimaginative. For a while, it seemed as though you were actually getting along with Grant. It's been quite boring." Ah, so the true Richie had shown his colors. She had growing boring again—apparently to both Grant and Richie.

He adjusted in his chair, leaning forward a bit, his eyes lit up in excitement. "But, if you were to drop out of the competition unexpectedly, right before the Golden Rose Ceremony—leaving Grant at the altar so to speak—I think that would make for some stellar ratings."

Ratings. She could have leapt across the desk and

strangled this man. He was the reason she'd stayed and got-ten her heart shattered all over again. And now he wanted her to leave, because it suited him. For ratings. She should stay here on principle alone. She would show him that she couldn't be controlled like Chris Legend, that she didn't bend to his every want and whim. But principle be damned. She wanted to go home. She wanted to pick up the pieces of her life. She wanted to drown herself in work until the pain went away. "That's it? I can go?"

Richie nodded, but held up his hand. "The only thing I need from you now is an exit interview with Chris. We'll air it on the Golden Rose Ceremony tonight. If you have anything at all to get off your chest, this interview would be your opportunity to do it."

An exit interview. A chance to get things off her chest. And then a flight home, to her comfort zone. To work and her apartment and her favorite coffee shop a block away. "You have a deal, Mr. Odom."

Chapter Twenty-Six

A single gold-plated rose rested on the pedestal on the veranda. The camera crew hadn't arrived yet, so Grant allowed himself to eye it with contempt. This show made this rose nothing more than a trophy. It wasn't symbolic of his undying love. It wasn't symbolic of his true feelings. It wasn't symbolic of his true choice.

Not that he had a true choice anymore.

He wanted Rochelle. He did. But he wanted *all* of her— something he would never have again. Which was what he deserved, he'd decided. No, he didn't sleep with Cassandra, but breaking up with Rochelle before he'd even let her explain herself had done the damage. That, and allowing Tiffany Wallace to fawn all over him so soon after their breakup. He should have been more stern with her at the time, and now he was paying for it because it had planted a tiny seed of doubt Rochelle would always have, a tiny seed of mistrust that would always be between them. Hell, if he hadn't dumped her so callously, he wouldn't even be on this show. He'd be with Rochelle somewhere on a beach, drinking something fruity and planning his next attack on her delicious body.

Tonight was going to be bad...

If he chose Maya, she was sure to reject him on national television. He wouldn't expect anything less from her. She was loyal to Rochelle and would perform her friendly duty, he was certain of it. But he didn't care about the show's audience seeing him humiliated; the only audience he cared about shocking was his mother, who truly had her heart set on Rochelle. Sharon Drake was expecting a happily-ever-after this time. And no matter who he chose, no matter how badly he wanted it, he wouldn't be able to deliver on the fairy tale.

The daughter-in-law she already loved was lost to her forever. And Grant had to be the one to tell her that.

A few of the cameramen meandered onto the veranda, interrupting his thoughts. One of them approached Grant to shake his hand. "It's been a pleasure working with you on the show, Grant," he said. "You've got one tough choice ahead of you."

"You're telling me."

"You nervous?"

Grant shrugged. "As much as any man would be, I guess."

"Cheer up. You never know what will happen." The man stalked to his camera, a grin on his face.

At first, it seemed like a throwaway remark. Then Grant remembered Chris telling him that Richie had a surprise for him tonight. *You never know what will happen.* Obviously the crew *did* know what would happen. Or at least, that was what they'd have him think. With Richie, everything was a mind game.

But didn't he already know what was going to happen, too? Of course he did. After all, he controlled how the show would end. And he knew the choice he had to make.

Chapter Twenty-Seven

Rochelle settled on her couch in her robe and slippers and cradled a fresh pint of Ben & Jerry's while fumbling for the remote control. She'd told herself she wouldn't watch the live Golden Rose Ceremony tonight, that she didn't care what happened now, and that moving forward involved her detaching herself from the show. But, she reasoned, maybe the final episode would give her some closure—closure that she never had ten years ago when Grant broke her heart for the first time.

Settling in, she took a big bite of the ice cream while she watched what seemed like endless commercials. Apparently the show had done well this season, garnering huge sponsors catering to the reality TV audience. Soon, the beginning credits of *Luring Love* began to roll and the camera zoomed in on Chris Legend, who introduced himself and Grant as he always did. Grant looked stoic, and a bit sad, and Rochelle reveled in the fact that maybe, just maybe she was the cause of his distress for once. That maybe deep down he realized what a complete jackass he was. *Wishful thinking*.

She tucked her legs underneath her, celebrating the fact that she was on the other side of the camera for once. It was going to be a two-hour episode; surely she could find something therapeutic in watching Grant make a fool of himself. On the flight home, she'd finally acquainted herself with what the Internet and media had to say about the show. Apparently after Cassandra's infamous admission, the audience was torn on whether or not Grant was truly a gentleman. It seemed that up until that point, he was a shoo-in from all angles. Now though, several blogs insisted Cassandra was a liar, while others claimed they knew all along Grant had a thing for the leggy blonde twin. She even found a website called Bachelor and the Beast which was solely devoted to reaching out to Grant to convince him to vote Rochelle off the show.

Chris brought her thoughts back to attention when he announced, "Before we begin, we have a rather shocking announcement to make. A contestant has dropped out of the competition as of this morning. Grant, I'm sorry to say, Rochelle is no longer one of your choices for the Golden Rose Ceremony."

For his part, Grant didn't appear surprised at all. Rochelle thought he might have nodded slightly, but otherwise gave no outward reaction. Disappointment swirled in her stomach. She didn't know what she'd been hoping for, but it wasn't that. She'd wanted him to be hurt, wanted him to betray his feelings on live national television. But maybe that was the problem. Maybe Grant couldn't care less one way or the other. Maybe Grant didn't actually *have* feelings.

"Before she left though, she had a few departing words for you Grant. Or should I say, a few departing words for our audience." Again the golden cart was rolled out with a large flatscreen television on it. Grant watched without expression as they turned it on. Rochelle took a huge bite of Ben & Jerry's and waited for her exit interview to begin. Richie had told her she could say anything she wanted, that nothing was off limits. And so she had literally told America everything.

"Hi, all," she began. "As you know by now, I'm no longer a contestant on *Luring Love*. But before I tell you why I dropped out of the race and forfeited my chance at winning the bachelor's heart, I have to start from the beginning. And the beginning starts when Grant and I were both in college together."

As Rochelle watched herself tell the story of how they'd met, how they'd dated, how they'd fallen in love, she was surprised to find that she smiled during those segments. That despite her pain, those memories still brought her joy. And she was surprised that she could see tears threatening to spill over when she spoke of their breakup so long ago. It had felt like a new wound as she'd said it to the camera just that morning, and it felt like a new wound now, watching from the comfort of her own home.

During the interview, the camera kept alternating between the television on the cart and Grant's expression as he stood there beside Chris and watched. He kept his hands folded in front of him, coming across as cold and unaffected. Rochelle took another bite of ice cream and waited for her next confession: the deal she'd made with Richie.

She told America how she tried to get voted off the show, how Grant had stubbornly refused, and how they'd fallen back in love—or so she'd thought—each while trying to outwit the other.

She wondered what Richie was thinking at that moment. If he regretted giving her free reign or if he'd wanted her to do exactly what she did, all for the sake of ratings. She decided she didn't care. The conclusion to her interview was drawing near. She didn't want to hear the words again, didn't want to think about them, but she couldn't stop herself from watching.

Closure, she thought to herself. *Closure*.

"Despite everything that happened years ago and despite his betrayal with Cassandra on the show, I'm still in love with Grant Drake. And that is why I couldn't come to the Golden Rose Ceremony tonight. I hope the viewer audience will understand. I can't ever face him again. Thank you."

And the screen went blank.

The camera whisked to Grant, catching the tail end of his reaction: Anger. What he could possibly be angry about, Rochelle couldn't fathom. *He'd* screwed *her* over, not the other way around. What, had he expected her to lie down and take it? Not this time, Grant. Not ever.

"Wow, Grant," Chris was saying. "You look a little peeved. It is because Rochelle's interview was so revealing? Tell us how you feel about all that has happened this evening. Did you think she would say the things she did? Do you have anything to say to our audience?"

But Grant only gave Chris a sharp look. A look that clearly said he was in no mood to play by the rules of the game. Chris recovered smoothly, as though he'd expected such a reaction, and smiled widely at the camera and

America. Rochelle wondered what there was to smile about exactly. She'd just compromised the integrity of the show—that is, if a show like *Luring Love* had any integrity in the first place. Wouldn't her accusations of bribery and unethical participation in the show make any producer sweat? Ah, but apparently not Richie.

Yes, Richie had definitely been hoping for her to spill her guts. Why?

"Well, it seems our bachelor is speechless for the moment," Chris said. "But as they say, the show must go on, right? So without further ado, let's call our final contestant, Maya, onto the veranda."

The French doors to the veranda opened and out stepped Maya in all her glory. Her navy blue dress was form-fitting and her hair was arranged in some fantastic creation of curls and braids that made her look like royalty. Rochelle smiled, despite herself. Maya looked gorgeous.

Chris strode toward Maya, placing a gentle hand on her shoulder. "Maya, you look lovely this evening. Tell us, with all the competition removed, how confident do you feel that Grant will offer you the Golden Rose?"

Maya smiled brilliantly at Chris. "Thank you, Chris. Before I answer that, I have something to say myself."

"Really? Do tell."

"You know, Chris," she said thoughtfully. "We all have regrets. We all say things we don't mean, or do things to embarrass ourselves, or act in ways we won't be proud of later. But I find that the things I regret the most are the things I *didn't* do. You see, I knew about Rochelle and Grant for a good part of the show. As soon as I found out, I should have backed out. I should have quit when I knew they still loved each other."

"You think they still love each other? What about Cassandra and her accusations that Grant slept with her repeatedly on the show?"

"Actually," a voice called from the French doors. "Those accusations are not true."

Rochelle nearly dropped her pint of ice cream as Cassandra strolled onto the veranda.

Chapter Twenty-Eight

Grant's jaw dropped as Cassandra strode over to him and placed a gentle kiss on his cheek. Chris smiled, very obviously aware that this would happen. Grant on the other hand, wasn't sure how much more of this show he could take. It was just a few acrobats short of a circus.

"Cassandra, welcome back to the show," Chris said. "You're looking as beautiful as ever."

"Thanks, Chris. It's great to be back. Especially under the circumstances."

Grant felt a coldness steal through him. What else could possibly come out of this woman's mouth? After the show, he would already be the country's most hated man, especially after Rochelle's emotional confession. Now what would Cassandra say? Had Richie concocted a false pregnancy this time? He wouldn't put it past that man. And what if Rochelle was watching? She'd said she still loved him. Surely he could win her back after the show—that is, if Cassandra didn't completely blow his chances.

Agreeing to be the bachelor for *Luring Love* was the worst mistake he'd ever made, he decided as Cassandra sauntered to stand beside Chris. She looked confident and pleased with herself.

"As Rochelle said in her exit interview," Cassandra was saying, "they had made up during their home visit to Grant's parents house. They officially became a couple at that point, and hid it from the producers."

"Yes," Chris said. "But what does that have to do with you?"

"You see, they weren't as good at hiding their feelings as they thought. So the producers came to me and explained the situation. At first I was really mad, because all of us wanted to take Grant home as our prize. Me and my twin sister were already fighting over him, and that's saying a lot. We never fight over anything, especially men."

"But why would the producers tell you about Rochelle and Grant? It seems like a weird thing to do, to expose their deal with them."

Cassandra nodded. "Richie—that's the guy who runs the show—he told me that by being all secretive about their relationship, Rochelle and Grant were robbing the show of ratings."

Grant's throat started to constrict. He slowly backed away from Cassandra. He'd never physically touch her, but yelling in her face was an overwhelming temptation at the moment.

"So," Cassandra said, "Richie said that if Rochelle and Grant wouldn't give the show drama, then the show would give *them* some. That's why I said I slept with Grant. That, and the money Richie paid me." At this, Grant's fists balled. "It wasn't close to the prize money, but it paid off my car. But you already knew that, Chris. You were there, remember?"

"Is that so?" Grant ground out. His eyes locked with Chris's. The show host took a step back from him, probably trying to decide whether or not to call for security. But right now, Chris wasn't important. "I've changed my mind," Grant said. "I have plenty to say for the final ceremony."

Chris swallowed, looking uncertain, but beckoned for one of the cameramen to zoom in on Grant. "Go ahead, Grant. America is all ears."

Grant took off his tie and undid the first two buttons of his shirt. Forget the dress code for this stupid show. All he cared about now was somewhere out there, hopefully watching this last episode.

He looked into the camera. "Rochelle, the moment our paths crossed ten years ago, I knew you were the one for me. That hasn't changed. Not after our first breakup, not after our second one. So much has come between us. So much that wasn't our fault." He pulled a small box from his pants pocket and opened it to the camera. "This ring is now ten years old. I've tried to get rid of it. To sell it, to give it away. But I could never bring myself to do it. I know why now." He closed the box and held it gingerly in his hand. "I couldn't give it away because it's yours. It's something that has always been yours and always will be yours. It doesn't belong on anyone else's finger, no matter if we're together or not. This is your ring, Chelle. And if you give me the chance, after all of this, I'd like to give it to you in person. I'd like to give it to you on bended knee, the way I would have all those years ago. You said in your exit interview that you still love me. I can't leave here tonight, without you knowing, without America knowing, that I love you, too, more than a man should be able to love a woman. So if you want to, if you have it in you, let's find each other after all of this. Let me show you how I feel, Chelle. How I've always felt."

Chris was standing beside him now, clapping him on the back. "Well said, man, well said."

Grant turned to his friend. "You're going to want to call security now. Richie's going to need a SWAT team."

"Cut!" Chris yelled, but Grant's hands were already on him.

Chapter Twenty-Nine

When the show suddenly cut off and went to commercial, Rochelle jumped from the couch, knocking her ice cream onto the floor.

Grant never slept with Cassandra. It had all been a set up. Every bit of it. He hadn't betrayed her. He hadn't cheated. And she had done the same thing to him that he'd done to her all those years ago—she'd refused to hear him out. She'd assumed the worse and cut him off before he could explain anything. All those times he tried to call, and she wouldn't answer the phone.

Oh God, she'd been so very wrong. So horribly stubborn.

She snatched her phone and dialed Grant's number. Over and over she tried to reach him but he would never pick up. She even waited until the commotion of the show should be over before she tried again to call. She called and called until finally his phone sent her straight to voicemail.

She would just have to wait for him to call.

No matter how hard she tried, Rochelle couldn't concentrate on the stack of work piled on her desk. She'd drank so much coffee she thought she might have a seizure, but all she could think about was Grant. All she could think about, sitting here in her office, was that she'd ruined her chances at happiness.

He never called back and still wouldn't answer her calls. She'd tried all morning, in between client meetings and phone conferences, but he never picked up. He had a right to be angry, but what about his closing speech? Had he made it up for show, to polish up his good-guy reputation once more?

Just then, her assistant Shelley flung her office door open and snatched the remote control from Rochelle's desk. "You've got to see this!" she said, changing the channel to the news. She turned up the volume so that the room echoed with the reporter's words.

The journalist on the screen stood outside the mansion where *Luring Love* had been filmed. Rochelle recognized the overhead view of the garden maze immediately. Still, it took a moment to comprehend what was happening. She focused in on the man on the screen. "The producers of the popular reality show *Luring Love* are suing the bachelor, Grant Drake, for attempted bodily harm to some of the crew and in particular, the show's host, Chris Legend. Drake, who is being held without the possibility of bail, was arrested last night for disorderly conduct and use of lethal weapons, since Drake's profession is tactical training consultation—"

Arrested! No wonder he hadn't answered her calls. After all Richie did to them, he had the gall to arrest Grant for his reaction? Oh *heck* no. Rochelle stood, her chair flying behind her and colliding with the bookshelf. "Book me a flight, Shelley. And get me a car to the airport."

Chapter Thirty

Grant lay on the bottom cot of the cell, arms tucked behind his head. Jail was decidedly boring. There was nothing to do but sleep, and that was a relief compared with all the free time he had to think about the events of the last two days.

His entire life had been put on hold simply because he'd scared a few people into their places. Sure, he'd hunted down Richie in the mansion and threatened to give him a black eye, and yes, he'd nearly busted Chris's lip open. And what was he supposed to do, *let* the security guards on the set stop him from finding Richie? So he'd had to evade them as well.

This point was, he didn't actually do any of those things, just threatened them—which was apparently still against the law.

Oh yes, he was in a world of trouble. But the worst part of it all was that he had no idea what Rochelle was thinking right now. Had things changed after Cassandra's confession?

Had she been watching him as he basically proposed to her on national television? Would she give him another chance? And why hadn't Colby found a way to get him out of this predicament yet?

The judge was apparently a good friend of Richie's and so had dealt Grant the worst deal. For godsakes, who ever got denied bail for starting a brawl? He'd been willing to pay a fortune if he could get out and at least call Rochelle. But they'd confiscated all his belongings—including his cell phone—when they'd booked him. These four tiny walls were driving him mad. He had a woman to go after, a future to pursue. He finally had a life beyond work, and these four walls kept him from all of it.

Down the hall, he heard the heavy metal door to the cell block open and shut. Probably another inmate being introduced to his new living conditions, which consisted of wafts of body odor and piss, hard mattresses, and zero privacy. The new guy was in for a real treat.

"He's this way," he heard the guard say. "The cell at the very end." Heavy booted footsteps preceded the click of high heels as the apparent pair made their way down the hall.

Grant sat up and waited. After all, *his* was the cell at the very end. And he had a visitor. His mother had said she would come see him, but he'd gotten a message through Colby to ask her not to. Apparently she hadn't cared about his request. Not that she ever did.

Still, he couldn't imagine his mother wearing high heels to a jail. She hadn't even worn high heels to his brother's wedding—which had pissed off her future daughter-in-law. It wasn't so much that she hadn't worn heels; it was more that she'd worn tennis shoes under her dress.

As Grant smiled at the memory, the burly guard plodded to stand before him. Grant leaned against the iron bars and grinned at him. "Well, Fred, so good to see you again."

"You've been released, Drake," Fred said gruffly, his mustache twitching with disgust. Grant had no friends here in the jail. Word had got around he was there, and apparently fans of *Luring Love* had gathered outside and picketed for his release, while news crews had set up camp everywhere on the grounds. The workers of the county jail had had quite the difficult time getting in to work each day, and they credited that little inconvenience to Grant himself.

Wordlessly, Fred stepped aside.

And there stood Rochelle Ransom. "I thought you could use a good attorney," she said. She gave Fred the once-over. "Well what are you waiting for? Do you need to read the judge's orders again? Unlock the cell before I have your job." She looked back to Grant and smiled. "We'll get your things and try to leave out the back. They're practically rioting out front, and I'm afraid I stirred up even more commotion when I showed up."

"Why are you here?" Grant said, following her like a puppy as she led him down the long hall of cells. She looked like a cop-devouring beast in that business suit and those heels. God, but she was gorgeous.

"I saw the last episode, Grant. All of it."

He grabbed her wrist and whirled her around. "But why are you here? I don't want your charity. I don't want your pity."

She looked at him for a long time. "I'm here for you, Grant. When I said I loved you, I meant it. And I can't very well have you if you're in jail. Now the charges are preposterous and won't stick. I've got my team working on the civil suit as we speak—"

But he didn't let her finish. He pulled her to him, covering her mouth with his. She melted against him, instantly ditching the all-business attitude and morphing into the soft, sweet Chelle of his dreams and fantasies. The Chelle he wanted to spend the rest of his life with.

She had come for him. She was here, and she was his. It was all he needed. Fred cleared his throat from behind them, and Rochelle giggled into Grant's lips. He pulled away smiling.

"Fred's shy," Grant explained.

She ran her thumb along his bottom lip. "Then we'd better get going before things get too steamy for Fred's innocent eyes."

The promise in her eyes had his body on fire. "Let's go out the front," he said. "Let's face the crowd. Together." It was a show of unity and a show of possession on his part, if he was being completely honest with himself. He was claiming Rochelle, and he was doing it publicly. He only hoped she felt the same.

Apparently she did. She smiled up at him. "Okay. Let's do it."

As they reached the glass double doors and the crowd outside came into view, he heard Rochelle take a big breath. "Here we go," she said. "Are we ready?"

"I'm ready for anything with you."

"Even…fans?"

"Let's think of them as friends. They're obviously happy for us," he said. "They're here for us. These are the people who have been watching us week after week, episode after episode. It would be wrong not to reward them for their loyalty, don't you think?"

She nodded. "They have signs that say 'Reunite America's Sweethearts.' I didn't know we were anyone's sweethearts."

He took her face into his hands and kissed each of her cheeks. "No matter what, we'll never let this get weird. Promise?"

"Weirder than it already was on the show? I promise."

They opened the doors and stepped out to the crowd, hand in hand. A deafening cheer reverberated through the throngs, echoing off the tall buildings surrounding them. The masses parted for them as they made their way down the stone steps and into the car waiting for them at the curb. Rochelle opened the car door and began to slide in, but Grant caught her and pulled her back. Before she could react, he got down on one knee.

The crowd went ballistic. Rochelle burst into tears. And Grant slipped the ten-year-old ring onto her finger at last.

Epilogue

Chris leaned against the wall in the hall of the hospital, arms crossed. Grant wasn't sure how he could be so calm at a time like this. "Relax, man," Chris said, as a nurse passed in the space between them.

"Relax!" Grant breathed. "My wife is having our daughter and you want me to relax?"

"She's not going to have her without you. We both know Rochelle. She'll kick the doctor in the nuts if he doesn't let you in to be with her. Let them get settled."

"The doctor's a woman."

"Titty twister then?" Chris offered.

Grant laughed. "I wouldn't put it past her." It was good of Chris to be there with him now. But it had never been Chris's idea to press charges, it had been Richie's, and Chris had refused to testify at the trial. Grant could even overlook past offenses he'd committed on the show. Chris had flown out here from Los Angeles to be with them while their daughter was born. And he'd sent Richie's camera crews on a wild goose chase so they could have some semblance of privacy. Everyone wanted to see *Luring Love's* first love-child.

"Grant! Chris!" a familiar voice called from down the hall. Maya strode toward them with the elegant grace of a ballerina, despite the Noah's Ark themed scrubs she was wearing. Rochelle had insisted on having the baby in the hospital where Maya worked because "only one pediatric nurse is good enough to care for *my* daughter." Grant was going to have a one-on-one with Maya about convincing Rochelle that they should see a pediatrician closer to their home, some six hundred miles away.

"Grant, where's your mom?" Maya said, giving him a friendly peck on the cheek.

"Her plane just landed. Chris is going to pick her up at the airport for me."

Chris nodded at Maya, his face taking on an ironic look. "Hello, Maya. Pleasure to see you again."

She grinned at Chris. "You didn't tell him, did you?"

He pulled an imaginary zipper across his lips. Chris looked a lot different in a T-shirt and jeans. He could have been any guy on the street instead of a celebrity show host. He looked a lot like the college friend Grant knew and trusted.

"Tell me what?" Grant said.

Maya sighed heavily. "I've decided to accept *Luring Love's* invitation to be on the show again."

"*Why?*" Maya had done well on the show—mainly because she wasn't a raving lunatic—but Grant considered her too good to be chasing after some man who probably didn't appreciate everything he had in her. Sure, the show had patched up his own love life, but he firmly believed he and Rochelle were the exception.

"Because this time, it's the bachelorette edition."

Grant felt his eyebrows raise. "That'll be…interesting."

Maya giggled. "That's what I'm hoping for. You only live once!"

Chris pretended to pout. "I tried to tell her she should just date me and forget the show. I even told her I'd relocate to… Where are we again?"

She poked him in the side. "Richie would never let you live so far from the set."

"Actually, I quit the show," he said, shoving his hands in his pockets.

"What? When?" Grant asked.

"About ten minutes ago," Chris said. "When Richie said he was sending a camera crew to the airport to film your mother coming through the gate. Sorry, man. He tracked us down somehow. Guy's crazy."

Grant cursed under his breath. He took out his phone to call in a warning to his mom, but the doctor opened the door beside him. "We're ready for you, Mr. Drake," she said. "Momma bear is a little grouchy."

Grant flashed a grin at Maya and Chris. "Here we go." He accepted the hospital gown and paper cap the nurse handed him. He looked ridiculous and felt amazing.

Chris eyed him thoughtfully. "What's the first thing you're going to teach your daughter? How to deliver an uppercut? How to palm thrust an unsuspecting attacker?"

Grant smiled at him through his too-tight surgical mask, snapping on the latex gloves. "I can teach her everything I know. But there's one thing Chelle will have to show her."

"What's that?" Maya asked.

"How to lose a bachelor."

He closed the door behind him, leaving his friends to ponder over that. Rochelle sat along the edge of the bed, panting and sweaty in her hospital nightgown. The nurse behind her looked at the monitor by the wall. All things electronic seemed to beep up at him.

"You're going into another contraction, Mrs. Drake," the nurse said. "You'll want to get back on the bed and begin your breathing. The doctor will be here any second."

"You," Rochelle said, giving Grant a scowl. She did as she was told, though, moving her legs to lie back on the bed. She even accepted his hand when he offered it to her, squeezing it hard. "After this is over, I'm going to harvest your testicles, pickle them, and keep them in a jar on my desk. Thump them every now and again for good measure."

He swallowed, not because of her threat, but because of the pain she must be in to make such a threat. In general, she usually adored his testicles. "Are the pain meds not working?"

The nurse shook her head. "She opted for no pain meds. Said she didn't want to dull the experience."

Dull the experience. It was one of life's most painful, and the thought of Chelle going through it without anything to buffer it made him want to vomit. Stubborn woman. He'd have to deal with this delicately.

"Chelle," Grant said, choked up. He could deal with a lot of things. But knowing the woman he loved was in pain wasn't one of them. "You should take some—"

"Says the man who won't take Tylenol after getting

twenty-seven stitches on our honeymoon!"

"Twenty-nine," he chided gently. "And it looked worse than it felt." They'd gotten rambunctious in their lovemaking on the private balcony of their beach cottage, and he'd ended up going overboard. He fell thirteen feet, and he'd ripped open his arm on the railing, but fortunately landed in the white beach sand. It had been the biggest inconvenience of his life. Rochelle insisted on being "careful" with him the rest of the honeymoon. She'd been furious with him for not taking the pain meds he'd been prescribed. Now he knew why.

Just then, Rochelle clenched her teeth. "I have to push! Where is the doctor?"

The nurse hurried to her side, lifting up the small blanket covering the lower half of Chelle's body bent at the knees. "She's crowning," she said, pulling on gloves. "I'm afraid the doctor won't make it in time."

Grant felt blood pool in his feet. This was happening. Rochelle was going to have this baby without pain meds or a doctor. Oh God.

Chelle screeched then, bearing down, and within seconds the nurse held his daughter, bloodied and bruised and beautiful, in her hands. It took Grant all of a breath of a moment to react. In one swift motion, he cut the cord, reveling in the fact that the baby was now out of his wife's belly and into their lives. Tears welled in his eyes as the nurse handed their infant girl to Rochelle, who was still shaking from the final push. "Grant," she rasped. "We did it."

He melted beside them both, planting a forceful kiss on Chelle's forehead and a gentle one on their baby's. Pride swelled inside him. His daughter had a head full of dark hair just like her mother and screaming lungs to match. He would recognize the Drake nose from anywhere, though, even if it was just a bit smushed from her journey. His mother would be elated.

Even though they were still at odds over baby names. His mother wanted to call her Elle, but Rochelle insisted that they would not have rhyming names and proposed Jocelyn. He personally didn't care what they named this tiny miracle now, as long as she was his.

"Have you ever seen anything so beautiful?" Chelle asked, after their daughter had finally settled in for some quiet snuggling.

Grant shook his head. "Nothing more beautiful exists."

Chelle leaned her head against his and sighed. "Eleven years in the making."

He chuckled. "Totally worth it."

She smiled up at him, radiant, but tired. "Totally. Maybe I didn't win that stupid dating show," she said, "but I ended up with my dream life. That has to count for something."

"It counts for everything. That dating show was no contest for us."

"And nothing ever will be."

But Chelle was already nodding off to sleep, with their daughter in her arms.

Acknowledgments

Acknowledgements are always the hardest part of the book to write because there are so many people to include and remember, but to be honest, with each new publication, there is always an easy one I can knock out right away: my agent. I can't ever thank my agent Lucy Carson enough for what she does for me on a daily basis. I have a serious agent-crush on her, guys. Seriously. For reals. No, really.

I want to thank Liz Pelletier for being a rockstar editor with this, for all her brilliant insights and for trusting me enough not to waste her time with this crazy book. Thanks to the Entangled marketing and publicity staff, especially Debbie Suzuki, for being so darn creative and wholly on board with my outlandish ideas at times.

Thanks to my critique partners Heather and Kaylyn, and to my authorly partner in crime, fellow Entangled author Ayesha Patel.

Thanks so much to my sisters Lisa and Teri who helped

me through some very difficult times that happened during the making of this book, and thanks to my family as a whole for always being supportive of my writing career.

And last but not least, thanks to my readers. Whether you're new to me, or you've followed me over from the Syrena Legacy series, THANK YOU! :)

About the Author

Anna is the *New York Times* bestselling author of the *Syrena Legacy* trilogy. She lives in Florida with her husband and daughter. She enjoys pranking random people, coughing loudly at inappropriate times, and drinking sweet tea. Especially the sweet tea part. She loves connecting on Twitter, but beware of her excessive use of sarcasm. Her favorite color is rainbow, and her writer's cat is a wiener dog named Puckledoo.

Made in the USA
Lexington, KY
25 November 2015